FEED THE HUNGRY ATOM

RICHARD B. CHRISTIE

Editor's Creative Media
5680 King Centre Dr #600
Alexandria, VA 22315, USA
info@editorscreativemedia.com

Ordering Information:
Quantity sales. Special discounts are available on quantity purchases by corporations, associations, and others. For details, contact the publisher at the address above.

ISBN (eBook):   978-1-952062-13-1
ISBN (Paperback): 978-1-952062-12-4

Rev. date: 03/21/2020

This book is dedicated to the memory of my brother
Robert who had inspired me to begin writing

CONTENTS

1 Tuesday, 10 April 2018, 8:30 A.M. Washington, DC Seven Days to Tax Day 1

2 Friday, 11 May 2018, Chen Chow Wan Restaurant East 4th Street, New York City, NY 5

3 Tuesday,15 May 2018, NASA Johnson Space Center, Houston, TX 9

4 Thursday, 17 May 2018, Shanghai Institute of Physics Shanghai, China 13

5 Monday, 21 May 2018, UNAG Offices United Nations, NYC 17

6 Friday, 18 May 2018, NSIU Headquarters, Washington, D.C. 21

7 Tuesday, 15 May 2018, Early Evening, Aboard a U.S. Naval Aircraft Carrier, 40 nautical miles south of Cyprus 27

8 Wednesday, 16 May 2018, United States Department of Energy, Germantown, MD 33

9 Thursday, 17 May 2018, Lattakia, Syria 39

10 Friday, 18 May 2018, UNAG Offices United Nations, NYC ...45

11 Three weeks later, Wednesday, 6 June 2018, Security Council Chamber, United Nations, NYC 49

12 Monday, 11 June 2018, Central U. S. Trucking Corporation Home Offices, NYC 55

13 Tuesday, 12 June 2018, NSIU Headquarters, Washington, D.C. 59

14 Tuesday, 12 June 2018, Tokomak Fusion Construction Site, Near Suzhou, China 65

15 Saturday, 16 June 2018, Hilton hotel, Washington, D.C. 71

16 Tuesday evening, 10 July 2018, Tokomak Nuclear Site Near Suzhou, China 77

17 Tuesday, 10 July 2018, Central Texas University, Faculty Housing Center, Austin, Texas 81

18 Wednesday, 11 July 2018, Ivan Nub's Restaurant, NYC...........85

19 Monday, 6 August 2018, Tokomak Nuclear Site,
Near Suzhou, China.....................91

20 Monday, 20 August 2018, NSIU Headquarters,
Washington, D.C.....................95

21 Tuesday, 21 August 2018, NASA Johnson Space
Center, Houston, TX.....................101

22 Tuesday, 4 September 2018, Trans World Shipping
Company Home Offices, San Francisco, CA.....................105

23 Monday, 24 September 2018, NSIU Headquarters,
Washington, D.C.....................109

24 Friday, 4 October 2018, NSIU Headquarters,
Washington, D.C.....................113

25 Monday, 7 October 2018, Hochog Ship Building
Company, Monrovia, Liberia.....................117

26 Wednesday, 17 October 2018, NSIU Headquarters,
Washington, D.C.....................121

27 Tuesday, 30 October 2018, Tokomak Nuclear Site,
Near Suzhou, China.....................129

28 Friday, 9 November 2018, General Secretary's
Office, Beijing, China 135

29 Friday, 16 November 2018, W. H. Ocean Shipping
Company, Offices, Hong Kong.....................139

30 Monday, 19 November 2018, NSIU Headquarters,
Washington, D.C.....................143

31 Thursday, 28 November 2018, General Secretary's
Office, Beijing, China 147

32 Monday, 3 December 2018, NSIU Headquarters,
Washington, D.C.....................151

33 0800 Tuesday, 11 December 2018, Aboard the
China Girl East, 1,644 Nautical Miles northwest of
the Panama Canal.....................155

34 Thursday, December 13th, 9:00 a.m., The United
Nations General Assembly NYC.....................159

EPILOG Saturday, December 15th, 1:00 p.m.,
University Chapel, Central Texas University, Austin, Texas .161

1

Tuesday, 10 April 2018, 8:30 A.M.
Washington, DC
Seven Days to Tax Day

Although it had rained last night, the sun had come out this morning and the Cherry Blossoms were in full bloom. The grass on the Capital Mall was becoming greener by the day, and the air had a fresh sweet scent that made you feel relaxed, and in no hurry to do much of anything.

Unfortunately, the nearby traffic was as noisy as ever. Most of the people, as they were walking along, were staring at their cell phones completely lost in their own little social world. None of them were paying any attention to what was going on around them.

Lieutenant JG Jane McCalla, from the United States Navy Special Investigation Unit (NSIU), neatly dressed in her crisp Navy-Blue Uniform, was sitting on a bench across the wide walkway by the Capital stairs. She had arrived early for a scheduled meeting at 9:15 A.M. with the newly elected minority representative from Kentucky's eighth district, Sally Martin.

Jane was anxious to meet her. She hadn't seen her for more than three years when, at that time, she was still a student at the University of Kentucky and Sally had been her Math professor.

Sally, just ten years older than Jane, had found that she was a natural in figuring out complex problems, and soon they became close friends.

When Jane graduated from college, with honors, and went off to the Naval Officer Training School, Sally had thought the Navy was going to get a super young officer. It had turned out much as she had thought, and within a year, Jane had been assigned to NSIU and became an assistant to Rear Admiral Harry Walker, the head of the unit.

Just last month, she was awarded a second one-half stripe and raised in rank from Ensign to Lieutenant JG.

It was Jane who was the first to call and congratulate Sally when she won the election last fall, and they had stayed in touch ever since. But it was today, after two years, that the young navy officer was to first see her friend again, now an elected representative of Congress.

Over at NSIU, Lieutenant Harold Jarrett and Chief Petty Officer Paul DeNice, sat across from Admiral Walker as they were reading through the action request that had been in the admiral's lock box that morning.

It seems a shooting took place in downtown Chicago yesterday evening that had targeted two city officials, both of whom had survived. The gunman, a tall man wearing a full helmet with a plastic shield over his face and gloves on his hands, had ridden by on a motorcycle, shot both men, raced off and disappeared around the corner.

The report stated that local police found the motorcycle, parked by a fire hydrant, five blocks away. It had been reported stolen from a parking lot, two hours earlier, and there were no identifiable markings found that would lead to who the thief or shooter was.

Paul looked up at Admiral Walker and said: "Why does the NSA (National Security Agency) want us to look into this? It would seem that the local and state police have a much better chance of finding out who did this than we would."

"That was also my reaction," said the Admiral.

He continued: "But I think they feel there may be a political entrapment involved. Chicago politicians, with their strong political malfeasance, have a reputation of showing a lack of support for law enforcement."

Turning his head to Chief DeNice he added: "Paul, would you take a look and see if you can find any ideas regarding a course of action, we might take with this?

Paul nodded and said: "Yes sir."

"On another subject," the admiral said: "We have received an inquiry from NSA, regarding a rumor they heard that the Chinese may be building a nuclear site near the city of Suzhou in eastern China. It is unconfirmed at this point, but they asked if we will please take a look and see what we can find out about it. Harold, would you check your sources and see if we can find anything about this?"

Harold nodded and said: "Aye sir, I'll look into it."

Paul asked: "I believe the only other open item we have sir, is this very unusual request we got from the State Department to look into a possible take down of a terrorist cell in Aleppo, Syria.

"That is usually in the province of the DOD (Department of Defense) and done as a joint action military strike along with our allies.

I understand it's the leader of the cell that is the target they want; taken alive if possible, but why us?"

Admiral Walker, shaking his head, answered: "I really don't know why; all I know is that this cell leader is a 'real bad Momma' who, it seems, also has a strong direct connection with Iran; and they really want to interrogate him. In addition, from what I've been told, he apparently has a big hold over the Damascus Ba'ath Party leaders.

That's all I know at this point, but while I get better answers, why don't you see if we can get a team together and have them set up and ready to go."

Dismissing the meeting, the admiral stood up and said: "I have to go over to the DOD for a meeting, so maybe get started with these and see what you can find out."

Both Paul and Harold stood as well, and Harold said: "Aye sir, we'll get on it."

Back at the Mall, Jane had walked over to the Capital and met Sally at the stairs and the two began their anticipated visit together over coffee in Sally's office.

2

Friday, 11 May 2018
Chen Chow Wan Restaurant
East 4th Street
New York City, NY

The smell of cooking shrimp, chicken and spices permeated the atmosphere of the small Chinese restaurant; actually, the smell was all around the neighborhood. It had wafted out the kitchen door and was caught by a light breeze that carried it to the street like a sensory advertisement for an exotic experience.

Emilio Watson sat and waited for his three other companions to join him at the small table near the rear of the restaurant. Every Friday, the four friends got together for a Chinese luncheon, with a pot of green tea and the special of the day.

They were late today, and he was getting hungry with that sweet smell from the kitchen. He hoped they would get there soon, because he had to get back to his office for a scheduled meeting at the International Ocean Shipping Company (IOSC), where he was director of Pacific Ocean shipping coordination.

The door opened, and a young man and woman entered; looked around, spotted Emilio, smiled and strode over to the table.

The young woman said: "Sorry we are late, but John and I got a last-minute phone call from Gene. He said he had to wait for a call from an investor in Switzerland who had been hearing rumors about food supplies in the Far East."

John Carrick and Annie Selene slid into the booth as Annie continued: "The Mercantile Exchange, as you well know, is rather slow moving; but unusual news from a foreign source can usually interrupt a sleeping dog."

John added: "Gene told us to go ahead and not wait for him. He told me that, with the time difference between New York and Luzern, he might not make it at all today."

With those very words barely spoken, Gene Elbridge walked through the door, came over to the table and slid in next to Emilio. Frowned at the others and said: "Sometimes I wonder why I ever listen to financial advisers!"

Emilio shook his head smiling and said: "Because none of us would have a job if they didn't exist!"

"I know", said Gene "but sometimes they just move so slow that a rock in the wind would pass them by, and other times they seem to think everything happens immediately.

"This Guy in Switzerland is a wealthy investor who usually trades in gold and silver futures. He had heard a rumor that the United States was probably going to take a big hit on a mix of agricultural products in the international trade market. So, as an arbitrageur, he wants to sell off two hundred contracts of twelve-month New York mixed agricultural futures and, at the same time, buy an equivalent amount of similar Shanghai futures."

John, who worked as associate director of a major trucking company that moved many of these food products to the West coast for overseas shipping, said: "Where did he get that idea from? That type of trade works with precious metals, not with perishable foods."

Gene looked over at him and said: "He didn't say; but said the world marketplace may change if what he heard from a European scientist is true. I tried to get him to explain, but he said to just get the trades done, and then hung up the phone."

Annie asked: "Did you get his trades done?"

Shaking his head, Gene explained: "I put the orders in, but the Shanghai exchange was already closed for the weekend; I placed the New York order, but without a lot of reason, the sale price just wasn't going to move very far. So, I called him back and told him that there wasn't anything else I could do. He said alright but, make sure I get it done first thing Monday."

Annie, a junior executive for a major international banking conglomerate, sat quietly and thought about what had just been said. She knew, as did the others, that a stray news item from an international source could have a dramatic effect, not only on the market, but almost everything.

She decided to look into all available references in regard to the trading of food production sources, and those that had been in any way affected by the trade balance between countries that involved the USA.

Knowing that it could be a difficult thing to determine, she still was wondering why a futures investor would risk so much money on an arbitrage order unless he had a really good reason for it. This type of action was usually done only by international banking investors who were really very sure of what was likely to occur.

The Chinese waitress, who had come to their table and taken their orders while they had been talking, heard what had been said. When she went to the kitchen to place the orders, she slipped out the back door, pulled out her cell phone and made a call.

Speaking in Chinese, she repeated what she had heard to the person on the other end. After a moment of silence, she heard the person she called say: "OK, I'll pass it on that it may be out!"

After lunch was finished, the four friends all went back to their respective offices and began to look for anything in the news, or for that matter anywhere else, that may have information related to the international trade of food sources.

In San Francisco, Wayne Hon, executive secretary to billionaire shipping magnate Harvey Wassel, owner of Trans World Shipping Corporation (TWSC), stood and wondered what he should say to his boss. Mr. Wassel did not always take unexpected news well; and the information he had just received, with the call from the waitress in New York, could be termed unexpected.

He stepped out the door into the bright California sunshine and walked over to his office to compose a report about the news he received. It would be on Mr. Wassel's desk when he returned from his golf outing later this afternoon.

Harvey Wassel returned from an early afternoon of golf at the Bay Golf and Country Club and stopped in at his office before heading home for the weekend.

He had a habit of always checking his mail late in the day, so as to always be sure everything was kept up to date and any problems or situations could be handled or disposed of right away.

He found the short report from secretary Hon, setting on the table, picked it up and read it.

Holding it by his side, his thoughts were of the communications he had had with several of the leaders of the Communist party in Beijing about the project near Suzhou, and what it could mean to the world economy.

He had been positioning himself for an agreement with the Chinese that would move most of his large shipping fleet away from the United States. He wanted to be ready to become the primary service provider for a projected expansion of the Asian market.

He was prepared to invest more than half his fortune to modify the majority of his shipping fleet. He would purchase additional ships, and by having them ready to accommodate the needed transport, and with having all the work done in China, he was looking at controlling most of the Pacific and Indian Ocean shipping. Also, his plan was to use Chinese crews to man the ships and to stop using the expensive union controlled American crews.

He went over to his FAX machine and sent a copy of the note to Beijing.

3

Tuesday,15 May 2018
NASA Johnson Space Center
Houston, TX

Katie Burns was looking at the latest aerial photographs that had been recovered from the Orbital Photo Lock Satellite (OPLS). It had slowed down over the past year, slowly losing its orbital speed until it passed through the atmosphere and crashed into the Gulf of Mexico yesterday morning.

The trajectory had been calculated and was well known, and a navy recovery team had been at the splash down location to recover what had not burned up upon reentry.

The OPLS had been in orbit for eleven and one-half years and was at the projected end of its usefulness, but NASA had been asked by the NSA to assure the recovery was accomplished.

The NSA had, for years, used the photo reconnaissance that had been available from OPLS, as the orbital flight path of the satellite passed over the northern hemisphere. That orbital path included all of Russia, Asia, and on down through most of the Mediterranean countries, and over the middle east; allowing them to keep an eye on many undisclosed activities.

The NSA did not want any foreign review of the knowledge that had been obtained while the satellite had been in service.

The photos were quite good, and very detailed. They had been taken at 360 second intervals with an extremely high definition lens and digitally enhanced. It was almost possible to read the license plates of the cars, on the streets photographed below.

The photos Katie had been looking at were some of the very last to be obtained from the satellite's final orbit. They had been taken as the OPLS passed over eastern China, across the East China Sea and then out over the Pacific Ocean.

She noticed a large-scale construction site northeast of the ancient city of Suzhou. As she got up from the review position she had taken and sat back, she wondered what on earth could the Chinese be building that would require such a large area.

She went over to the tracking computer data recovery program and searched for the last previous time the OPLS had passed over the exact same point. It took a few moments to recover the data point; and she found that it had been approximately fourteen months earlier. When the photo from that time and data point was retrieved, it showed only a large hilly plain made up of farm fields, a few rice paddies and rural houses with dirt roads.

Katie copied the old photo from 2017 and a print out of the photo from yesterday, marked them for NSA eyes only and put them in a secure transfer envelope to be sent off to Washington.

The next day, when the envelope was received at NSA, the review agent was just as puzzled as Katie had been. He, however, passed it over to the scientists at the security center and they got quite excited about it.

It was quickly understood what was being built. For that size and shape of construction, there was really only one explanation. The large flat land and the circular perimeter structures being built around the edges could only mean one thing; the Chinese were building a 'Tokomak Fusion' reactor and particle accelerator.

Although the principal behind a Tokomak reactor has been around for some time, the cost of construction and, with the usable output very questionable, the science behind it was usually kept in a classroom environment.

'Fusion' nuclear reaction joins particles together, and 'Fission' splits them apart. The real advantage of Fusion, in the nuclear generation process, is that the radioactive half-life decay time of the fuel waste for Fusion is very short when compared to that of Fission.

It is, however, theoretically possible to generate enough power for it to be almost self-sustaining. A free particle released by the fusion process, while passing at high speed through multiple magnetic fields, will act like a transformer and generate an electrical output.

However, as a primary electrical source for mass consumption, the efficiency had always come up just a bit short. That, and when coupled with the high cost of construction and potential operational hazards, it was usually considered to be impractical.

It therefore had mostly been relegated to the advanced study of theoretical science. The most famous and widely known Tokomak in the world is found at the French-Swiss border facility of the European Council of Nuclear Research (CERN) in Switzerland.

There, the large particle accelerator and large 'Hadron' particle collider is used by scientists, from around the world, to advance their theoretical knowledge on how the universe was formed.

There are of course a few other Tokomaks, small in comparison, and located in several different countries. But they are usually just too cost prohibitive to build. Several times, they have been built to provide energy to various area electrical grids, but the output was always just a bit too short to be practical.

Standard nuclear generation facilities, found in many locations around the world, function by using fission; an action that generates tremendous heat. That heat is used to make steam that drives turbo generators; a proven and efficient way to produce electricity.

So, why would the Chinese build a Tokomak now?

Why, with a struggling economy, would they spend so many resources for so questionable a return?

Because of its nuclear capacity and its unknown projected use by the Chinese, the NSA decided to ask the investigative team at NSIU to work with the CIA (Central Intelligence Agency) and look into how and why the Suzhou facility was being built and who was behind it.

Since the Chinese could not deny its existence, and with their strong participation and position in the United Nations, an additional request was sent to the United Nations Action Group (UNAG) asking that they look into it as well. With the presence of a new nuclear component being built by a powerful member, they needed to determine if an action recommendation should be provided to the Security Council for consideration.

4

Dr. Lin Chang Lee, director of the fusion project, was sitting at his desk, upstairs in his Shanghai office, reading over the last report he had received from the directors of scientific development in Beijing. They were informing him that knowledge of the fusion project near Suzhou may have leaked out and it was now going to be difficult to keep it quiet.

They had been a little skeptical at first, about the actual viability of the particle accelerator project, and thought it would only be time before they must explain its potential to the world. However, the political drivers of the communist ruling party surprised him by jumping on to the idea quickly.

Dr. Lee understood their questions, but there were several new potential advantages that had been brought forward; surprisingly, in a very different arena than that of weapons or energy production. The theory that had been advanced was actually in mass food production, and that was what surprised him about the politics of it.

From information that Dr. Lee had obtained at an international shared symposium and conference in Hong Kong almost two years ago, he learned that researchers at CERN had found that particle acceleration and isolation of an electron, from several different types of plasma fuel, left a combination of unusual and unstable protons and neutrons (*Quarks*) behind.

The researchers at CERN had been concentrating on particle acceleration and collision results, for the alteration or creation of either matter or anti-matter; and, thus were overlooking what was left behind in what could be, and usually was, called waste.

They had, however, found that when certain combinations of these waste products were put together, the resulting combination of Quarks simply rendered them stable enough to place safely away in storage.

Several other scientists, when looking for a viable use for these stabilized waste products, found that when combined with certain molecules from both animal and vegetable products, they would substantially accelerate the growth of proteins within those products.

Dr. Lee had thought the result, if proven, could possibly alter the way mass production of the Chinese food source was provided.

Beijing was well aware of the food shortage problem within its own country and throughout Asia as well. But with a population of 1.4 billion people, they would always be looking for a new and better economical source that could occur within China. However, when Dr. Lee presented this theory to Beijing, it was the additional potential of exporting large quantities of high protein foods that became the driving force behind their interest.

If that could happen, then the international economic trade balance could tilt strongly in China's favor; and that would be a strong driving force. If they could become the primary provider of food to many poverty driven countries in Africa, southern and western Asia, and the middle-east; it would strengthen the power and control they would gain on the world stage.

At the international shared symposium and conference in Hong Kong, a scientific representative from Turkey, Dr. Sami Jallo, had been seated next to Dr. Lee at the discussion. He was pleasant enough, and soon Dr. Lee relaxed somewhat as they spoke to each other.

Later, they went into dinner and sat together at the assigned round table with six other members of the symposium group from South Korea, Japan, Australia, India, Greece and Jordan.

Conversation was light and mostly in English which, maybe not too surprisingly, was the most common language at the table. They spoke of their families and home life, and a little of the science they had seen earlier that day. Over an excellent dinner with fine wine, they all relaxed and got along quite well.

Somewhere in the conversation Dr. Lee mentioned his daughter, Lijuan, and her strong interest in history, ancient people and archaeology. He was very fond of his daughter and, at 23 years of age, she reminded him of his lovely wife who had died of cancer just three years previously.

Dr. Jallo, himself a strong history buff and family man, said he would be happy to sponsor Dr. Lee's daughter with her studies of the ancient 'Levant' region (the larger eastern Mediterranean) including the 'Hittite' and 'Egyptian' peoples from that ancient time period. The area Dr. Jallo spoke of, happened to be the exact area that Lijuan had been studying in preparation for her master's degree at the Beijing Institute of History and Archaeology.

When, two weeks later, her father spoke to Lijuan about the sponsorship offered by Dr. Jallo for her studies in Turkey, she got very excited. It was, after all, the very area of study she was so interested in.

The arrangements were made and, with approval from the course professors in Beijing, she flew off to meet with Dr. Jallo in Ankara. He had arranged that she could continue her studies, of that ancient area, with an archaeological research team from the Turkish historical preservation department.

For more than ten months Dr. Lee got an e-mail or letter from Lijuan twice a week. They were filled with excited descriptions of artifacts and the ancient people that she was coming to know as if they had existed today. An occasional e-mail from Dr. Jallo, assured him that he was keeping an eye on her well-being.

The fusion project had been moving along well, and there had been little conversation regarding its progress. Dr. Lee was, however, torn. The way site construction was progressing, and with unnecessary bureaucratic pressure from Beijing; his goal of increased food production was actually suffering because of the construction itself.

The method the Chinese use to build such a project was simple. The Beijing authority, following previous mass development projects built in Shanghai, Zhongshan, Guangzhou and other developing areas, sent teams of recruiters to the remote countryside to attract and hire hundreds of very low-income men, women, and children who they would then move to temporary housing units built on the perimeter of the construction area.

They were enticed by being given twice their previous income and also provided temporary housing for them and their families.

By putting several experienced building engineers, mechanics and craftsman in charge of large teams of laborers, they could move through the mass development at a quick pace.

The problem with this socialist form of obtaining laborers, is when the project was completed, they don't want to return to their remote homes or previous lifestyle.

Now that they had become accustomed to an enhanced way of life, but with no longer a need for their continued labor, it created a political problem. The state was now faced with a sizeable quantity of untrained and unemployed laborers and their families.

They became a drain on the local economy and, by not returning to their fields and farms, caused a national decrease in mass food production, and the loss of remote labor as well. Unemployment increased and poverty soon followed along with it.

Dr. Lee, realizing that the scientific level of expertise was going to be continually more and more intensive as the structures became completed, was concerned as to where these educated technicians and scientists that were needed would live.

The temporary housing was not a long-term solution, and the nearby city of Suzhou could only handle and support a fraction of the necessary people.

However, there was a new, very modern, rail system that could handle the increase. He hoped that the availability of upscale homes in commutable range would entice these people to move to the facility.

But now, the stress on him was to get it built and proven. He was risking his reputation and his scientific connection with Beijing on this. He was also concerned that other, less informed, political Beijing bureaucrats would look at this facility and realize that they were actually getting a nuclear site that could be used for different causes having nothing to do with food process and production.

5

Monday, 21 May 2018
UNAG Offices
United Nations, NYC

Sally Kirk, a senior representative from the UK, walked down the corridor from her office to the conference room and saw that there were fourteen members of the committee already sitting at the table. She had been named UNAG chairman of the group just three weeks ago and was still a little unsure of how to act.

Moving to the middle of the table, she sat down and smiled at everyone and said: "We have a new item that was received just this morning that we need to review. It is, perhaps, a little strange in that it concerns a permanent member of the Security Council.

"We have received photographs taken from a satellite just four days ago, and also 14 months ago, over the same area that shows a very large construction site located in a northeast corner, near the city of Suzhou, in eastern China."

She took out her file and passed around copies of the photographs and the scientist's opinion.

She continued: "As you will see, the photograph is very high definition, and shows the construction is on-going. The construction site is unusual, and several nuclear scientists, in the United States, believe that it appears to be the beginning of a Tokomak Fusion Particle Accelerator."

She smiled at everybody and said: "I have absolutely no idea what that is, but it is the opinion of renowned nuclear scientists, so I am sure it is important.

"This just arrived, so we have not had any conversation with China's representative, and they are unaware of our interest as we speak.

"As we all know, nuclear facilities of any kind are within the province of the UN, so we must notify the Security Council of this when we can be assured of its accuracy."

A French representative spoke up: "A Tokomak is a very special kind of nuclear physics in that it uses fusion rather than fission in the production of energy. Although very advanced and safer, it has never been economical enough to be useful. The most famous fusion facility in the world is at CERN in Switzerland."

The Swedish representative joined in saying: "I understand that the use of such a facility is more for the use in education than in practical use; so why would a country with a very large struggling economy like China spend its money on this?"

Sally spoke up: "I ask each of you to take the copies of information you have and please do some research about this. With the international nuclear proliferation agreement, it is important that we know what it is and what it can do. We will reconvene on Wednesday at 2:00 p.m.

"In the meantime, I will ask the representative members, who have nuclear facilities in their countries, for any additional information they may have that could help guide us in a recommendation for the Security Council."

As Sally returned to her office, her telephone rang and when she answered it, she was surprised to find the Chinese UN Ambassador was calling her.

With a translator on line, the ambassador said: "I understand that UNAG has been advised of a construction project we are building by the city of Suzhou. Perhaps I can be of assistance to your committee.

"The satellite photograph of our construction site is, in fact, a nuclear fusion production site. We knew that the project would be known about quickly, and it has so been determined.

"The project is not for weapons, but for a scientific development that we found may have a useful purpose for the waste product of fusion materials and could provide significant gains in the production of high protein foods. We believe this process may help us to feed millions of people in our country."

Sally, very impressed but also very cautious with the candid statement from the ambassador, answered: "Thank you, Mr. Ambassador for your clear explanation of the project.

"I am sure you understand that, because of the nuclear agreement, we must present our findings to the Security Council. With your permission, I believe we should also provide a written copy of this telephone conversation along with the notification."

The ambassador agreed with the UNAG chairwoman and said that he would be pleased to cooperate.

After Sally hung up from the ambassador's call, she sat back in her chair and began to think about what she had been told.

All within one day; the discovery of a major nuclear project was uncovered in a member country, the call for a UNAG committee meeting to discuss the project and begin looking into it was made, and, almost immediately, was followed by an 'unheard of' telephone conversation with the member's UN Ambassador.

Although the UNAG Committee was there to review potential items for presentation to the Security Council, it almost never had a member state provide an answer before being officially asked.

Sally, at 48 years of age, was well past the acceptance of a coincidence such as had just occurred; and knew someone, perhaps a member in her committee, had notified the Chinese ambassador's office after the morning's meeting. She was, however, under an obligation to notify all of her UNAG committee members of the ambassador's phone call.

As she thought about it, it actually made it a little easier for her, for now she could openly discuss it.

However, when a committee member over steps their sworn duty and leaks an item that is under consideration, the very existence of UNAG was compromised.

She needed to know who the leaker was!

It was really pretty obvious, one of the committee members is from China; and was probably well aware of the project before it had even been presented.

In all probability, the call from the China ambassador had been planned for some time. It would make sense that there would be a detailed explanation already figured out to release when the project was discovered.

The basic information regarding the discovery, had been provided by the United States NASA organization, to the US Ambassador under confidential dispatch, and following procedure, was directly forwarded to UNAG.

Sally sighed, there was really no way that security of the project was not already compromised, too many people knew about it.

It was now up to them to find out what was really going on as to the reason for this project; and, if possible, find out how much it could influence the nuclear proliferation agreement. That is what UNAG needed to know for presentation to the full Security Council.

6

Friday, 18 May 2018
NSIU Headquarters
Washington, D.C.

Admiral Walker arrived early and grabbed a cup of coffee as he walked over to his office.

It was always a surprise, for anyone who didn't know him, when they first saw his office. You would think that an Admiral and head of an independent department of the navy would have a large office, with a big desk, maybe a sofa, some comfortable chairs, and neat as a pin; this was not the case here.

It was a small office, but it did have a large desk, a comfortable desk chair and two simple soft back chairs for visitors. The desk had three telephones one laptop computer a wired intercom, and usually about ten or so unimportant folders spread around.

It did have one window on the western wall, uniquely with a nice view, but with one-way glass; he could see out, but no one could see in. The picture on the wall was of his last command ship, an air craft carrier of older post Viet Nam era vintage. It had been scrapped five years previously.

On a small table by his door was a steel lock box with a small LED light on top. If the light was green, the box was empty; if it was red, he needed to open it and read the contents right away.

The admiral's investigative unit was a special unit made up of four officers, including himself, three civilian special contract employees, three Yeoman (secretaries), and eight enlisted US Navy Seal field investigator operatives.

Although they would frequently work with the CIA or the FBI, they were separate from both and other active naval units. They were under the direction of the NSA and used as a high security special action investigative group.

Although the NSA was a part of the Department of Defense (DOD), the Admiral's group was also frequently used as a legal investigative unit and for law enforcement under direction from the Department of Justice (DOJ).

This morning as the admiral, coffee in hand, stepped into his office he saw the lock box light was red!

When a quiet 'Oh Damn' slipped out of his mouth; he placed his coffee on his desk, walked to the lock box, entered the combination, opened the top and drew out the secure file from within.

The file contained several aerial photographs and several pages of written type. He looked at the photos first and wondered why he was looking at satellite images of a construction site. The written page told the story of the potential nuclear facility in China; but had little information regarding the high security reason he had gotten the file. Usually this type of inquiry was in the venue of the CIA or FBI.

The Secretary of Defense had attached a hand written note to the file, saying he thought there might be a lot more to this than what was shown and that he had made a phone call to the Secretary of State.

Because of current negotiations between the United States and China, they decided to direct the NSA to have the admiral's team look into this and find out why they are building it, and who was in charge of it, in China. That way, the CIA and FBI would not be perceived as infiltrating into a potential international nuclear situation.

The admiral thought that he had heard and talked about the possibility before; it was a rumor about a month ago that had prodded their interest, but they had been unable to get any confirmation about it.

As he sat reading through the file for a second time, Petty Officer 1st Class Ira Jones knocked on the open door and looked in. The admiral looked up and said: "Come in Ira what do you have?"

Ira, always the sailor first, stood straight, saluted the admiral, and handed him the faxed copy of a UNAG query that had arrived just fifteen minutes ago.

Ira said: "Good morning sir, NSA just forwarded this fax that came in from UNAG about a new nuclear site near Suzhou, China."

Admiral Walker said: "Sit down and tell me what it says."

Ira read it aloud. It said that UNAG had been notified by NASA of the new high-tech facility being built and was just beginning to look into it when a phone call, made by the UN Ambassador from China, came in; and he gave them a detailed explanation for the entire project.

Ira, looking up from the file, said: "Sally Kirk, from the UK, has taken over as UNAG Chair for the next six months and is a bit skeptical.

"She wants to know why China would expose such a secret project, all of a sudden, with such detailed and mundane reasoning."

The admiral said: "Sounds like she is smart. Actually, the notification of the project was in my lock box this morning. I had just finished reading through it when you came in.

"It seems the NSA wants us to look into it as well. Although things seem a little better in our relations with China, in the words once said by a former president, 'Trust but Verify'.

"Run it by Paul, he spent some time in that region about six years ago. Do some research and maybe see if we can check with MI-5 (UK intelligence) in London for any knowledge that they may have.

"I agree it is a bit unusual for the Chinese to do something like this and then openly tell the world about it."

Ira got up to leave and turned back to the admiral and said: "I understood that the president was working on better trade relationships with China, I wonder how this would impact that? Possibly that may be the reason for our involvement; how do we set this up, sir?"

"Good point Ira, go over it with Paul, but we will keep it low key for now; I'll ask the secretary if he knows," said the admiral.

Chief Petty Officer Paul DeNice was sitting sipping coffee at his desk when Ira walked in, grabbed a cup of coffee for himself, sat down and handed Paul the file he got from the admiral.

Paul, having been a part of the Seal Team 6 for nearly seven of the past nine years, didn't say anything; just reached over took the file and began to read through it.

When he studied the photographs, he looked up at Ira and a bit surprised, said: "Their building this next to Suzhou? That doesn't make much sense. It is a beautiful ancient city largely still existing in the old ways of China about forty years behind modern times.

"I remember back in college, I had a few scientific courses in nuclear physics, but they were very basic. You took some of those courses as well, didn't you?"

Ira said: "I took them, but never really understood them all that well. I like things I can see, not tiny particles floating around in magnetic fields doing things to other tiny particles floating around in magnetic fields."

Paul laughed and said: "According to the UNAG report, the Chinese ambassador says that this project is a result of their determination that it can improve food production.

"I wouldn't say that is not possible, but since it is nuclear, we need to find out a lot more about it.

"Also, if the Secretary of Defense sent this over, and he wants us to find out without telling anyone, it is probably a concern of the White House and their on-going negotiations with China."

He sat back and said: "I guess we best start with finding out where this nuclear food production idea came from.

"Who are the physicists in China or, for that matter, anywhere else, who would follow the path of discovery that would create such a project? I believe that most of the studies along these lines come from research done at the CERN facility in Switzerland."

Ira, thinking about it, said: "We are a little light on people at the moment; Luigi, Antonio, John, Carl, David and Rudy are all over on a carrier near Syria cleaning up after that terrorist they caught. However, I do have a thought.

"Luigi told me, some time ago, that he has some family in northern Italy that he hasn't visited in a long time. I believe it is in Verbania on the shore of 'Lago Maggiore' very close to the Swiss border, and not far from Luzern.

"Do you think we can come up with an idea, or excuse, to have him go and visit his family as a cover for a trip over to CERN and ask some questions?"

"I don't think so," said Paul, shaking his head; "We haven't gotten his report on the take down of the terrorist yet, so they are still out of it. Anyway, who would he ask to see that would give him the answers we need, and how would we get him in?

"I think that maybe we would do better going through our own scientific community at this time. Maybe we can learn what they may have noticed but just didn't think about enough to get involved with."

Shaking his head side to side, Paul smiled and said: "I remember the few times when we needed some information from these scientists; it wasn't always easy to get them to think on our level."

He laughed and continued: "Do you remember the meeting you and I had with the project manager for a NASA recovery building in Mississippi a few years ago?

"He was helpful and very intelligent, sitting there in his conference room, wearing a three-piece suit he was the very vision of an informed project leader. That was until he stood up to leave the room and we noticed he was completely unaware of the fact that he had no shoes and two different socks on his feet.

"Somehow their minds just get on a track that has no off ramp; that, and you are never really sure what planet they are currently on."

Ira said: "I guess you are right. Why don't we ask Lieutenant Jarrett for his input and maybe he, along with Lieutenant JG McCalla, would go and talk to some of our own NASA scientists to see if they can find out anything."

Paul smiled stood up and said: "I like that idea, Jane McCalla, with her sharp mind and pleasant disposition, could charm the snow off an iceberg; and Harold Jarrett just keeps digging in all directions until very little, if anything is left unknown. Let's go ask them!"

They found Lieutenant Jarrett sitting in the conference room with Linda DeSanto, one of the three civilian employee contract investigators. She had been previously a Vermont State Trooper and is now a great asset to the navy investigative team. They had been going over a possible Wall Street inside trader incident that may or may not have occurred in New York City just the other day.

Paul and Ira, as sailors do, stood straight at the open door and knocked for attention. When Harold looked up, Paul asked if they could possibly interrupt their discussion.

They were good friends with both Linda and Harold and had worked closely with them on a number of occasions.

With no objection from either, Linda got up and said she better be getting on her way up to New York anyhow, and with her very pleasant and sweet smile said good bye to them all and left.

Paul handed the file to Harold and gave him a quick sketch of the China Nuclear Food project with the questions it raised. They had wondered if he was maybe available to contact the science community and see if he could find out exactly what they were talking about.

Harold lifted an eyebrow, looked at Paul and said: "This sounds familiar, didn't we talk about something like this about a month ago?"

Paul said: "I think we discussed something about a rumor the Chinese were doing something nuclear, but we never did get any confirmation about it, maybe this is it.

"Anyway, we were just tasked with this and are going to need a base line understanding of what it all means. Our thought was, if Jane McCalla was available, that maybe you and she can dig into the scientists and find where or who this concept came from."

Harold said: "A lot of this doesn't make sense, but I admit nuclear physics is not my field; but it is interesting. I'll see if Jane is available and, if so, we will come up with a plan to see what we can find out."

7

Tuesday, 15 May 2018, Early Evening
Aboard a U.S. Naval Aircraft Carrier
40 nautical miles south of Cyprus
Eastern Mediterranean Sea

Petty Officer 1st Class Luigi Larenti was the leader of the current active strike group for 'United States Navy Investigation Unit – Seal Team 6'.

They had just completed taking down a terrorist cell in Aleppo, Syria that had been creating havoc over a six-block area of the northeast part of the city. It was in an area occupied by Kurds and not currently under the control of the Arab Socialist Ba'ath Party of Syria.

In an unusual request, the team had been brought in to take out and neutralize a specific terrorist cell; it was upon a request for help from the occupying Kurd Rebels, and because of the potential connections the terrorists had with Iran.

With reluctant acceptance, the American forces, along with a coordinated Kurdish effort, had been successful in the joint operation.

American intelligence had determined that the leader of the cell, who was recovering from a bullet wound to his left leg, was one of the top planning leaders for the entire Muslim terrorist movement in that part of Aleppo and Northern Syria. He also had very direct communication ties with Iran.

The NSA had learned of the cell's location and importance from a US Army intelligence report that had been obtained from a captured fifteen-year old female cell member. She had been sexually abused and forced by many of the men in the cell.

"

Stepping outside for some fresh air, and because of morning sickness, she was caught easily. Her movements were awkward and slow, and since she was about five months pregnant, she was very scared. Her being missing from the cell went unnoticed by the remaining terrorists.

The Iranian connection was the driving force; and the decision was made to have the NSIU - Seal Team 6 go in and neutralize the cell, with the desired intent to capture alive, if possible, the leader.

The strike planning was good. The information obtained from both the Muslim girl, and the Kurdish Rebel forces, was reliable and helped to locate and describe the building and its surrounding area to be targeted.

The Kurdish Rebel command allowed out several communication leaks that had led the terrorist cell to believe they could use the area residents as human shields.

The plan was simple; a small staged confrontation, about a block away, cleared most of the people from the streets. The Rebel Army then released a rumor that the remaining few soldiers, left behind, would only be needed as observers.

The terrorists were taken in by the quiet and relaxed atmosphere and decided to make a move on those few soldiers who were still there.

What they didn't know, was there were two divisions of Kurdish Rebel soldiers under cover surrounding the area. When the twenty-two terrorists from the cell moved in on their targets, they were trapped on all sides and virtually wiped out. There was no mercy from the Rebel soldiers, the terrorists were ripped apart to the man.

The captured girl had indicated that the leader was always under protection by four special lieutenants. She told them that they never left him alone and that he very rarely left the building. It was the neutralizing of these men that was the first goal of the Seal Team.

They arrived, wearing 'Thawbs', local clothing that covered them from head to foot. It hid their weapons and weapon-proof vests in the loose material and sleeves.

It went as their years of training and skills had prepared them for. When they got confirmation that the Kurdish Rebels had engaged and taken down the terrorists that had attacked the area, they moved at incredible speed entering the building and were confronted by two of the lieutenants who they immediately and soundlessly dispatched.

David, Carl and John remained by the entrance to back up the other three men as they quietly moved through the building checking the rooms.

When Antonio, Luigi and Rudy entered the last room at the end of the hallway, they caught the leader and his two remaining men completely off guard. They were taken down to the floor; bound, tied and gagged before they even knew it.

It was as planned, and not a single word had been spoken by the Seals. So good was their training, they had accomplished their goal and had the leader and two lieutenants in their custody without anyone the wiser. The cell no longer existed.

After a quick search of the building, they had taken their prisoners, and what additional intelligence they found, back to the aircraft carrier using the same helicopter they had used to get into Aleppo. There, investigative specialists would then interrogate the prisoners in detail. They would find out whatever they had planned, and where any other terrorists were.

Back on the carrier, in the debriefing room, while the team was beginning to relax after the capture, Lieutenant Commander Johnson, a navy intelligence officer, stepped into the room and said: "As you were," and asked: "Have any of you heard of anything about several foreign citizens, including an American, being held the by a terrorist cell in Lattakia, just over the Turkish border on the west coast of Syria?"

He was well aware that this Seal Team was under direct control of the NSA; and he had previously wondered exactly why they had come after this particular cell leader in Aleppo.

Luigi looked up at the intelligence officer with a slight frown, and said: "No Sir, our instructions were to take out this cell in Aleppo and take the leader alive if possible. That is what we did!

"We had no further instructions or information regarding the take down of any other cell. However, if you have information that we can help you verify, and the NSA approves, we are already here and can look into it."

The officer looked at each of the six men in front of him and thought, to himself, he didn't ever want to be on the wrong side of these men.

1st Class Petty Officer Rudy O'Neil turned towards the officer and with a very soft gentle voice, always surprising the first time anyone heard him, said: "Sir, did you say that another terrorist cell is holding and American and other foreign citizens captive? Do you have any idea who?"

The Lieutenant Commander turned and, relaxed by the low gentle voice of Rudy's question, said: "No Petty Officer, we don't know who they are. But the questioning that has begun on the terrorist leader got that out of him almost as if he wanted us to do something about it right away.

"Of course, his cell was in contact with the Ba'ath leadership, but contrary to popular belief, they keep things well apart from each other. There are a lot of mixed relationships amongst the different groups here, and actually, this cell was closer to Iran than Damascus."

Luigi, fully aware that the conversation was a little out of their current objective, said: "Sir, we will be in satellite contact with our division command in about an hour. I will advise them of this item you brought forward, and I will ask them to contact your group command for verification. If they wish us to get involved, we will of course, comply. At this point sir, we just don't know enough to be of any real help."

The Lieutenant Commander, nodding, agreed and thanked each of the team members for their participation in taking down the Aleppo terrorist cell. He got up and left to go back to his office.

The six men in the room sat quietly looking at each other. Rudy said: "Why did he come to tell us about these captive citizens?"

2nd Class Petty Officer Carl Muskin, who was new to the team, looked thoughtfully at Luigi. After graduating college, and with a master's degree, he had been a history professor at Central Texas University (CTU). That was until he found, one day, that sometimes history could be more accurately learned if one was actually a witness to it; so, he joined the navy and began his seal training.

When asked why he would ever leave the education field, his answer always was: "I never did!"

Carl asked: "Luigi, are you thinking of how an event, such as we just learned, could change things?"

Luigi smiled at Carl and said: "We shall see when I talk to the admiral. But I believe that he will want to know about it, he is a strong believer in the unusual and an American along with additional foreign captives, in Syria fits that bill!"

An hour later, Luigi had just finished his report to Admiral Walker when he said: "That is it Sir, that cell is finished.

"However, when we got back here to the ship, a Lieutenant Commander, who is part of the interrogation team, came to tell us they learned of several foreign civilian captives, including an American, that are being held the by another terrorist cell in Lattakia. That is just over the Turkish border on the west coast of Syria. It seems they got that information out of the terrorist leader very easily."

The admiral was quiet for a few seconds then said: "You know Luigi, I have always believed in coincidence, and maybe this is just too close. It probably isn't related in any way at all, but my stomach is rumbling again.

"If you and the team are safe and comfortable for a couple of days, I am willing to authorize you to stay there and take a look at this and see if a reason can be found.

"I'll notify Mediterranean Command that you are there to assist, and I'll talk to the NSA to see if they have any knowledge of this. Please, if you can, remain a bit separate from any interrogation effort of the Muslim cell that you took down; but as usual, Luigi, use your best judgement, guided by experience, and I will have your six."

8

Wednesday, 16 May 2018
United States Department of Energy
Germantown, MD

After making about ten phone calls to various scientific centers, Harold finally found the one who knew what he was talking about was located at the satellite building for the Department of Energy (DOE), in Germantown, MD. The director of nuclear research was Dr. Charles Cootes, and his secretary made an appointment for 1:30 p.m. that afternoon.

Jane McCalla and Harold Jarrett, in their crisp navy white officer uniforms, drove up to Germantown for a meeting with the man they hoped would put them on the road of discovery to what was behind the Chinese Tokomak project.

As they arrived at the entrance they were cleared through and directed to the small office building at the end of the long driveway. They parked in the designated visitor parking space and walked over to the door.

It was a very small lobby and the secretary, who had been waiting, stood up and welcomed them. She said that Dr. Cootes was on his way back from the research lab and would they please follow her to the conference room, he would join them shortly.

About five minutes later, a very tall thin man with fiery red hair and a goatee walked into the room, dropped the papers he had in his hand, tried to catch them before they flew all over the floor, and missed. All flustered, he said: "Oh damn, now I will have to start sorting them all over again."

Harold, with a small smile on his face, immediately stooped down and began to help him collect his papers.

After getting himself together, Dr. Cootes said: "That was a hell of a way to start a meeting with Navy Security." He sat down and continued: "I am Charlie Cootes and I understand you have some questions about a Tokomak being built in China."

Jane spoke first: "Thank you Dr. Cootes, I am Jane McCalla, and this is Harold Jarrett, we are from the navy investigation center in Washington. And, yes, we are looking for some information about, whatever you called it, being built in China."

Harold laughed and sparked a smile at Dr. Cootes as he said: "Please forgive us doctor, our area of expertise most assuredly is in more mundane things than nuclear physics.

"However, we have been notified that the Chinese are building such a facility near the ancient city of Suzhou."

Jane picked up the discussion and said: "We had discovered the project from satellite photos, and it was very quickly confirmed by the United Nations Ambassador from China.

"As I am sure you know, national security requires that we know where any nuclear facility is located, and what use it is intended for."

Harold picked up the narrative: "That brings us to why we are here asking for your help. When the report from the UN came to us, the explanation was that the Tokomak was part of a process to increase food production and not as an electrical supply or weapon source."

Jane said: "I don't know much about such things, but I understand that a Tokomak is a fusion process that joins atoms or parts of atoms together, so how does that help increase food production?"

Dr. Cootes smiled and said: "I see! Well, I think I may be able to help out a little bit about that.

"About two years ago, there was a symposium and conference in Hong Kong that was presented by a group of research scientists from CERN in Switzerland. It was part of the biannual scientific exposition that they sponsor.

"At the Hong Kong meeting, the CERN people were working on accelerating an electron away from certain materials in an effort to create a new form of matter.

"That was the primary reasoning for the presentation, but they also had a few researchers there who had worked with the waste part of the material after the fusion process had occurred.

"Those researchers, while trying to stabilize the remaining plasma, found that when it is exposed to certain animal and vegetable molecules, it would substantially increase the production of proteins in those items; and it had the added benefit of fully stabilizing the remaining plasma."

Jane said: "I think I understand what you just said, but I just wonder how an atomic particle by joining with another atomic particle, could increase food quality and production."

Dr. Cootes said: "Don't feel bad about that, the majority of attendees, including myself, had a similar reaction. That, and the fact that the cost of building such a facility is so great, most of us didn't see that the cost vs. benefit ratio could ever work.

"Apparently, the Chinese either found a better source of money or are taking a huge gamble with it."

Harold asked: "Is there any other good reason you can see for the building of this facility?"

Dr. Coots raised his eyebrows and looked over at Harold and said: "That, sir, is an excellent question. In the fusion process, one result is the releasing of free electrons and neutrons; it leaves them free to accelerate, within magnetic fields, to incredible speeds.

"There are even some theories that have been advanced, stating that if they can be straightened and passed through a 'laser' lens, with the resulting induction of free photons, it could create a destructive beam so strong it could destroy or pass through anything it hits at almost any distance."

Jane, taking a deep breath, looked directly into the doctor's eyes and exclaimed: "You have got to be kidding!"

Dr. Cootes smiled and said: "It is only a theory at this time; there are many obstacles that have never been overcome. For example; the maximum speed ever obtained by any sub atomic particle is very close to the speed of light, never exceeding it. Also, we know that a light beam, as a true mass, bends when affected by gravity, amongst many other problems."

He smiled at the two navy officers and said: "Relax, we too have many theories; some are practical, and some are just imagination. The one I just described to you falls in between. In theory, it is possible but with so many obstructions in the way, not likely. First of all, you need to have a Tokomak to create the free particles, and then they must be contained in a magnetic field, etc., not very portable."

Harold said: "So are we back to the food production theory?"

The doctor laughed and said: "That, or they are trying to generate a renewable electrical grid source, perhaps both!"

"OK, so who in China would we want to look at to figure out what they are doing, would you know?" asked Jane.

Dr. Cootes replied: "There are several scientists who are knowledgeable; but when I was at the symposium, I did meet with Dr. Lin Chang Lee. I suppose he would be a good starting point.

"Dr. Lee is a member of the Beijing scientific research community and has his offices in Shanghai. He was at a different table than I was at, but we did speak together for few minutes. He was fascinated by the food enhancement possibilities.

"He was the only one there from mainland China, but there were about fifty or so scientists from all over the world present. You may find it useful to ask CERN for their input and maybe get their guest list."

After thanking Dr. Cootes for his help, Jane and Harold headed back to their office in Washington.

Jane was quiet as they road along southbound on I-270, with many thoughts in her head. As she looked out the window, she said: "You know Harold, I wonder if we may be over thinking what the Chinese are doing with this facility.

"Dr. Cootes may well have been correct when he said they may be trying to generate a renewable electric grid source and, at the same time, solve their food production problem."

Harold said: "That may be, but the cost of construction is so huge; and with only a theoretical final result, why would they do it?"

She looked at him and answered: "That is what I mean by 'are we over thinking it'. Let's try this; we know that the construction cost of a nuclear facility like this is enormous. That is why we ourselves have not gone overboard with the idea. We also know that the electrical grid output, by most standards, is still below an acceptable value.

"These assumptions are based upon our economical view and the cost vs. benefit ratio for construction as we see it. But our economy is very different from the Chinese economy. For example, the average American's annual income is about 28,000 US dollars a year, and the average Chinese annual income is equivalent to about 12,000 US dollars a year.

"So, assuming they are efficient in their construction costs, the labor cost of building this facility is less than one-half what it would cost to build a similar one here."

Harold looked over at her for a moment, and said: "Yes, I understand what you are saying, but there are a number of other factors that could be at play here as well."

Looking back to the highway as he drove, he continued: "Although we know the electric grid part is inefficient, and the food part is still largely theory, they are actually proceeding with the project."

Jane answered: "I follow what you are saying, but there is another factor involved, and that is their population. The US population is about 325 million and the Chinese population, at 1.4 billion is more than 4 times that. So, with a population that size, a potential increase in food production is going to outweigh inefficient electrical grid production."

Harold answered: "So you think the economic risk is worth the attempt to gain a superior food source?"

She answered: "I certainly wouldn't dismiss it. Also, if it proves effective, it could affect any nation's food import-export business; including ours."

Harold asked: "What do we know about Dr. Lin Chang Lee? I haven't ever heard of him before, albeit there really is no reason that I should have.

"I think we now have sufficient justification to do some research on him. Apparently, he is well known in the scientific community, so if you will look into him, I'll see what I can find out from the people at CERN."

Jane said: "Sounds like a plan."

9

Thursday, 17 May 2018
Lattakia, Syria

The five people sitting together in the plane locked room were upset, uncomfortable and scared. They were in a small room with a wooden table and five wooden chairs; there was a small primitive bathroom with a curtain off to the right-hand side, one very small window, and the only door to the room was closed and kept locked.

After an uncomfortable trip in the back of an open dump truck, they had been forced to walk across a small field, behind a medium sized block style house, to an old one room block building with its back against a stone wall that surrounded the whole property.

They had been in the room for three days with only two meals, placed inside the door each day, made up of corn meal and some sort of unknown meat that had been burned on an open fire. There was a bucket of water and a cup they had to share. Each had been provided with a blanket to sleep on. Nothing else, and nothing was ever said or explained whenever their captors opened the door, to bring the food and water.

The archaeological research team, from the Turkish historical preservation department, had been doing a new study in Hattusa in Anatolia (modern Turkey).

The five researchers were headed by the British archaeologist Ralph Woolf, and consisted of advance students from France, Germany, the United States and China.

The students were Danielle Chartier from France, Albrecht Deaggs from Germany, Herman White from the United States, and Lijuan Lee from China.

They had all been down in a dig together looking at a carved stone serpent head that Danielle had uncovered just an hour before, when suddenly, eight masked terrorists appeared in the dig and grabbed them. They were quickly tied and gagged, lifted out and dumped into an open back truck. The site was then abandoned when they drove out and raced south towards the border with Syria.

Riding across the border on a remote dirt road, they avoided any contact with either Turkish or Syrian authorities.

An hour later, they were at the small storage building where they were locked in the single room, across from the large fire damaged house that, still habitable, had obviously been abandoned by the previous owner.

The terrorist cell leader, in Lattakia, was looking to establish a stronger base reputation and was actually in competition and conflict with the cell leader in Aleppo. They had calculated that if they could take an international hostage team from adjoining Turkey, the world's blame would fall on the Aleppo cell and the Syrian government.

They were making plans to video the execution of the captives when they found that the Aleppo cell had been destroyed.

Now, though by no action of their own, they had achieved their goal; they were likely to be recognized by other cells as the new ISIS leader in Syria and solidify their ties to Iran. They didn't think anyone knew about their hostages. So, they thought they might be in a good position and get even more recognition and influence.

The Lattakia cell location was known by the local authorities and had been easy to defend from attack by the local militia because of the stone wall surrounding the property and the sympathy of the local Muslim clerics.

They felt they were gaining strength. They figured that they could publicly execute the hostages to show their undisputed power. They calculated the most impact would be if it was done on Saturday. With their egos intact, albeit inflated, they let it be known that they would provide a show to explain their power.

Back on the carrier, Lieutenant Commander Johnson, with a thick file folder in is hand, called a meeting together in the briefing room aboard the carrier and asked the Washington seal team members to attend. Also, there were three special operation officers, and the ships executive officer Commander Isaac McCall.

Lieutenant Commander Johnson said: "Thank you all for attending this briefing, particularly the members of the seal team.

"I believe, Petty Officer Larenti that you have received confirmation from Admiral Walker that we requested your assistance with this unforeseen situation that has come to light. I am, of course, referring to the captive citizens now being held by the terrorist cell in Lattakia that we learned about from the interrogation of the Aleppo cell leader."

Luigi answered for the team: "Aye sir, we have received instructions to aid in this potential extraction, or needed action, in any way you feel we can be of assistance."

Lieutenant Commander Johnson smiled and said: "Thank you, we do need your help. Lieutenant Steve Gerrin is one of our special operations officers who has been following the terrorist cell's activity, and I ask if he will continue with the briefing and describe the known details regarding the Lattakia cell location and what details are known."

Lieutenant Gerrin said: "I am honored to be with you men and would like to add my thanks to both you and your commander, Admiral Walker, for your participation in this operation."

If you will look at the file copies of the known information and data that is in front of you, maybe we will see if a plan of action can be established."

For the next four and a half hours both the officers and the seals studied everything known about the target cell, and the possibilities of accomplishing a successful safe extraction of the captives.

It turns out that the Lattakia cell operation had been well documented and surveilled. There were multiple photos of the buildings and surrounding landscape that had been taken by drones in the past few weeks.

A live drone was currently over the site area far enough away not to be seen but close enough to monitor current activity. A live video from the high definition camera aboard was currently showing on the seventy-two-inch television screen in the briefing room.

A plan was put together that showed a night time raid was what was needed, so that the eighteen known terrorists would be in the main building and could probably be contained with both an air strike from a drone and a helicopter landing inside the wall to surround the building and keep the captives isolated and safe.

They knew that there could be a political outcry and complication if they didn't notify the various home countries of the captives, but they also knew time was of essence, so they relied upon the fact that one of the captives was an American. It would be Luigi, Antonio and Lieutenant Gerrin who would be responsible for getting the captives out and onto the helicopter.

The plan was prepared, and everybody was ready to go that night. The authorization from the DOD wasn't even questioned, so it was a clear go.

All went exactly as planned; the drone rocket, that was fired at the main house, was perfect and took down the remainder of the house with the one shot. The rest of the extraction was smooth and complete.

The team had landed, spread out and secured the wall around the compound. While Rudy, Carl, and John searched the remains of the house for survivors, David covered the exit route to and from both structures and the helicopter. The rooms had been blown apart from the drone strike and the roof caved in crushing anything beneath it. There were no survivors.

Lieutenant Gerrin, Luigi and Antonio went to the door of the store house building. Lieutenant Gerrin knocked once on the door and raising his voice, said: "Back away from the door we are going to break it down."

With that Antonio kicked the door open and pushed through. They found the five people huddled together in the far corner of the room.

It was Luigi who said: "We are from the United States Navy and are here to get you out to safety." Pointing to Antonio, he said: "Please follow this man and we will get you out."

Lieutenant Gerrin, took several photos of the room, checked for any additional information and nodded to Luigi to close it up.

The whole time on the ground was only eight minutes. The cell was completely neutralized, the captives were all safe and the helicopter, with everyone aboard, took off and rose quickly up and out of Syria. Twenty-eight minutes later, they were landing on the deck of the carrier.

Medical staff met the helicopter and quickly took all five civilians immediately down to the ship's hospital for a complete examination and physical checkup.

The team and Lieutenant Gerrin headed down to the debriefing room to complete their reports. Luigi put through a coded satellite link to Admiral Walker and told him all went well, and they were ready to come home.

Admiral Walker said: "You know Luigi, my stomach is still rumbling. I understand the international complications that are involved, but I have a strange feeling that we should split the team up; and have one of you, as an escort and for security reasons, travel with each of the survivors back to their individual home country embassy or their homes and families."

Luigi, quite surprised by this, said: "Aye sir, if I understand, you would like to know exactly who and what each of these student researchers are, is that correct?"

The admiral answered with a thoughtful pause: "I guess that describes it pretty well. Luigi, there is still that funny feeling that I have, that somewhere we are going to find a connection that we didn't think was involved in anything else we are looking at. I don't know what it is, but I don't want to let go quite yet."

"Aye sir, if you will clear it with Mediterranean Command and have us all flown off the carrier to Athens, maybe tomorrow morning, I can send one of us with each of the civilians to assure their protection, and escort them to their respective embassies.

"They all speak fluent English of course, but John speaks French and can go with Danielle Chartier, David speaks German and can go with Albrecht Deaggs, and Carl speaks some Chinese and can go with Lijuan Lee, and Rudy can go with the archeologist, Ralph Woolf to the UK embassy. Antonio and I can bring Herman White back to the USA with us."

Admiral Walker said: "I like it Luigi, do it that way. I'll get it all confirmed right away and cleared through the State Department and Mediterranean Command."

Early the next morning, the navy flew the team and the rescued civilians to the NATO base in Greece and then one travelled with each of them to their respective Embassies.

All went well, and the civilians were becoming fast friends with the Navy seals. After getting all the paperwork and the appropriate transfers done, at their own home country's consulates, they all decided that they would like to have a fine dinner together that evening at a famous Athens restaurant.

Ralph Woolf wanted to buy the dinner for everyone, but Luigi told him that the U.S. Navy would buy this one by saying: "Our commander was so pleased that we were able to get everyone to a safe place so quickly, that it would be his honor to provide the celebration dinner."

All enjoyed the evening, but especially Carl Muskin and Lijuan Lee; ever since they first saw each other, they both felt a very strong attachment between them.

The fact that both were deeply involved with the study and love of history, gave them a strong reason to exchange their ideas of the distant past. Each wanted to learn from the other about the discoveries they had made that transpired through the ages. It was, however, only one of the reasons they were so fond of each other.

Although the evening was pleasant, it also was short. Everyone had their own plans to go to their individual homes, and the Seal Team had a late-night MAT (Military Air Transport) flight scheduled to get them back to Washington, DC.

With an exchange of personal addresses and phone numbers and promises to keep in touch with each other, they all went their separate ways.

10

Friday, 18 May 2018
UNAG Offices
United Nations, NYC

Sally was at her desk, in her UNAG office, reading over the staff reports that were submitted by the various committee members at the 2:00 p.m. meeting on Wednesday.

The reports were all over the place with opinions from the different scientific communities from each of the member's countries, but all kept referring back to the CERN meeting in Hong Kong more than two years ago.

No one would say that the results were not possible, but neither did they say it was a good idea. They all agreed that the Fusion process was, by itself, less threatening than a Fission facility; but nuclear was nuclear.

An inquiry to CERN had produced, basically, the same result. Theory said it was a good idea, but they had not proceeded with it because their efforts and budget had been, and still are, in 'matter and anti-matter' creation from acceleration and collision of particles.

Those researchers who had looked into the effect caused by what the resulting Quarks created, were still in the discovery stages; albeit they were sure it was viable.

They were pleased and fascinated by the thought that China had picked up on the theory and was proceeding with building a Tokomak but, stopped short of stating its practical performance capability.

She had a note on her desk that she needed to send the recommendation report over to the Security Council today.

She picked it up looked at it and sighed.

She really had no choice but to prepare a recommendation that China's nuclear project was actually indeed, a full-blown, nuclear proliferation site. Therefore, under Council rules the China member must provide full disclosure and site access would be required.

As a courtesy, she placed a call to the Chinese ambassador and told him of the recommendation.

He answered: "We understand the UNAG recommendation and have prepared answers for it. Please do not concern yourself about sending it to the full Security Council. As soon as it appears on the schedule, we will bring our scientific experts to New York and have them present the project details to the Security Council.

"I ask that when that takes place, you will please join us at the presentation."

Sally sat back a bit surprised and said: "Thank you Mr. Ambassador, I appreciate your kind invitation, but that would be improper, and I must decline."

The ambassador said: "I really only meant for you to meet Dr. Lee when he is here, I think he can explain very clearly what we are doing and the potential it exhibits. I know you have spent a lot of time researching this theory."

Sally said: "I would be honored to meet Dr. Lee, and hear his explanations, but I must still send over the report as we currently have it prepared."

The ambassador said: "By all means, send it over, we expect it and will answer it as needed. Thank you and good day Ms. Kirk."

Sally sat quietly at her desk and pondered what had just occurred. The food enhancement project the Chinese were proceeding with was, in their mind, already positioned for action, yet some of the best and most informed scientific minds in the world are still looking at it as theory. What was happening would be exciting except it involved nuclear proliferation, and that makes it, possibly, dangerous.

She decided to document everything that she knew, including a print out of the tape from her phone conversation with the ambassador, and send it off to the United States NSA. They were the ones who brought it to them in the first place.

She called for an appointment with the head of the Security Council and took her committee's report over to his office and officially submitted the UNAG recommendation to the Council.

The secretary for the Security Council chairman, who got the official recommendation from Sally, signed and stamped the receipt and handed it to her. As soon as Sally left, the secretary opened the recommendation and read through it. She then resealed it back into its envelope, carried it into the chairman's office and handed it to him.

As she walked back to her own desk, she stopped and picked up her purse and left the building. Two minutes later, she was on her cell phone speaking to Wayne Hon and telling him all about it.

Although he had been expecting the news, it was still a jolt to know that it had now occurred. He knew that Mr. Wassel would have some reaction to the news and took his note book with him as he walked over to the billionaire's office.

"Okay Wayne," said Harvey Wassel, "it is what we expected. Now I need to assure our contact in Beijing that we will remain faithful to our agreement. Send a fax to Secretary Lieu, saying that we are still prepared to honor our commitment.

11

Three weeks later
Wednesday, 6 June 2018
Security Council Chamber
United Nations, NYC

A lot of questions had been asked and answered, with multiple inquiries to CERN, NASA, AEC (Atomic Energy Commission), and many international nuclear equipped countries. The universal opinion was a basic agreement that the construction of a Tokomak Fusion reactor and Hadron collider was very expensive and complex with little chance of economic reward.

Many of those who had heard of the CERN food enhancement program were on both sides of the fence.

While they all agreed that the possibility of producing high protein foods was a desirable factor, to this date, no one had actually shown it would work in large quantity. Those who thought it could work were still thinking in terms of the high cost it would take to prove it, others wondered what other use the facility could provide, other than an insufficient electrical grid source.

Dr. Lin Chang Lee, along with Beijing Assistant Defense Secretary Chen Hui Sing, and three assigned cabinet officials, Liu Gen Feng, Fu Li Meilin, and General Dong Chao Jing made up the Chinese delegation that would come to the United Nations and explain the project to the world.

Dr. Lee, with much pressure and pleading from his lovely daughter Lijuan, happily caved in and brought her along to New York City along with the delegation.

He knew, because she had told him, all about her time in Turkey and their capture by the Muslim terrorists from Syria. He was, secretly, very thankful for the quick and successful rescue mission by the United States Navy, whose immediate and decisive action saved her life and the lives of all her associates.

When the Beijing defense department was advised of the rescue mission, they wanted to be angry that the United States had risked the lives of all the captives without first advising them. However, they had to admit that time had been very short, and the captives were made up of international members, one of which was an American. So, the official acknowledgement sent to the United States State Department was polite and grateful.

Dr. Lee, however, knew his daughter better than she thought he did; and was sure her strong push to go with him to New York was because she had wanted to see the young man who was with the rescue team that saved them. He knew that it was a lot more than just to say thank you again. He had noticed that they had sent many letters and e-mails back and forth to each other over the past few weeks.

So, having never before traveled to the United States, he agreed that she could come along and that they would enjoy the sights together for a couple of weeks. Lijuan was thrilled, and immediately sent off an e-mail to Carl telling him she was coming to America.

When the delegation arrived in New York and, after checking in at their embassy, they got settled in at their various hotels. Lijuan, very excited about being there, walked out of the hotel and placed a cell phone call to Carl to let him know she was in the United States.

In Washington, after getting the call from Lijuan, Carl sat back and began to think. He had been very happy to hear from her and, at the same time, wondered exactly how this growing close relationship between them was going to work out.

He had no doubt that it was the sweet beginning of what could be a long-term thing, but he was an active duty U. S. Navy Seal and she was the daughter of a Chinese Government official.

It was obvious that a conflict between countries, on the diplomatic level, could quickly become a strong possibility.

He had now been in the navy for more than four years and, at the age of twenty-nine, realized that if this relationship with Lijuan was going to have any chance, he needed to make sure it wasn't going to compromise anything he was doing. So, with much thought, he made his decision, and with his future in his own hands, walked down the hall and knocked on Admiral Walker's door.

Admiral Walker listened as Carl explained the situation that was developing between, he and Lijuan. He then simply asked Carl what he thought they should do.

Carl said: "I am not sure sir, certainly Lijuan and I have a growing personal relationship between us, but I fully realize that my position in the U. S. Navy would be seen as a conflict in priorities; and I cannot allow that to happen. It could easily be pointed out that we don't even know each other all that well, however even our simple relationship, as it stands, is unacceptable to my continued active duty service in the navy.

"So, sir, my active duty enlistment time expires this month and, although I had planned to reenlist for four more years, I believe it would be best for me to, if possible, end my active duty in the navy and return to my teaching career, as a history professor at CTU.

"That way, regardless of what happens in the future, I would not be a hazard to anything that involves my country, the navy or my reputation; all of which are very sacred to me."

Admiral Walker sat silently and looked at Carl for several moments. He did not underestimate the courage or patriotism Carl had just displayed. This man had just placed his country's values before his own personal future. Although a military tradition, it was rare to see someone make such a strong life decision and also quietly show such courage. After all, it was based upon an uncertain potential of a life changing relationship.

He said: "Carl, I understand your position, and I admire your courage for bringing it forward. You are correct, of course, that a decision to leave the navy before anything happens is the right one, and I understand what it took for you to come forward and speak to me.

"I will assure that, with the sufficient time you have already served, you will receive an honorable discharge, and all earned honors and benefits of your enlistment, shall be transferred to your veteran status.

"It will be necessary for you, of course, to have an FBI review of your security status however, and that your clearance will be downgraded because of your potential personal association with a foreign national. That would be standard procedure in your service completion.

"Please know Carl, that we here at the investigation unit are, regardless of rank, a family and we care for each other as a family. You, as an important member of this family, have elected this very proper course of action and it will not alter our feelings or support. I'm sure you know that we all applaud your choice and will stand behind you all the way."

Carl stood and said: "Thank you sir, with your permission, I shall prepare all unfinished documentation and reports that need to be done and submit them to Lieutenant Jarrett. I am at your service and call until you have me released." With that, he stood at full attention and snapped a salute to the admiral.

The admiral with an unusual show of respect, also stood up and at attention returned the salute.

Back in New York, Dr. Lee was preparing the speech that he would present to the Security Council on Friday. He knew that there would be scientific disagreement with his conclusions, but he truly believed in the potential of his project.

The fact that he had many detailed conclusions from multiple scientific communities that supported his food enhancement program, many members still questioned it; particularly those who had had experience with Chinese promises before.

However, he could only present facts and theories that showed results that he believed.

He was a little uncomfortable, because he had been instructed, by the Communist party in Beijing, to take with him specifically, Fu Li Meilin and General Dong Chao Jing as part of the delegation to the United Nations. They were both from a group of power-hungry members of the party and would apply pressure whenever they thought they would strengthen their political position.

So far, they had not said anything, but it had been their original input position that the nuclear facility was large and to be built near Suzhou.

It was Assistant Secretary Chen Hui Sing, as the head of the Chinese delegation, Liu Gen Feng, director of the agricultural department, and Dr. Lee, the overall project director, who would be the ones slated to present the project details to the General Assembly at 10:00 A.M. Friday morning.

Assistant Secretary Sing gave the overall presentation to the Assembly, saying that it was part of China's responsibility to the world to establish new and modern procedures.

Lui Gen Feng was there to explain the anticipated increase in food production along with the packaging and distribution that is anticipated for the very poor and remote areas throughout Asia and the Middle East.

It was, however, Dr. Lee's presentation that everyone in the scientific community wanted to hear. He explained the theory that had driven the project and the potential value of it in the world marketplace.

The international reception of the Chinese explanation was, for the most part mixed. Most thought that the potential for increased food production and quality was a good idea, but many were worried that the construction of the facility was a rush to judgement as to its actual performance.

Meanwhile Fu Li Meilin and General Dong Chao Jing spent time meeting with the representatives from Honduras, Costa Rico, Nicaragua, El Salvador, Columbia, Panama and Venezuela. They were telling them some of additional potential that could be gained from a powerful new nuclear site so close to the east coast of China.

They were set to assure those representatives that the proposed Chinese assistance in Central and South America would be more reliable and secure than what was provided with their association with Russia, Cuba, and Iran. A big part of their argument was that China already had an established sea coast with many ports that could supply shipping more securely.

While they had their meetings with those country's leaders, they held the correspondence from Harvey Wassel close to their vests. It would be his shipping power that could be the hammer to come down on their resistance should they not agree; but they didn't need to know that now.

12

Monday, 11 June 2018
Central U. S. Trucking Corporation
Home Offices, NYC

Associate director John Carrick sat at his desk and looked at the pleasant young woman sitting across from him and said: "I don't understand your question Ms. DeSanto, did you say that there is a possibility that we are somehow involved with an act of espionage?"

Linda shook her head smiled and said: "Oh no Mr. Carrick! What I said is that we have some unverified information, that has surfaced, indicating several negotiation changes in international shipping contracts are being shared with unauthorized foreign agents.

"My asking you about it, is only to know if you have heard anything that might help us determine if the rumor is true. And, also to ask if you know of any major changes that occurred, that you can advise us about, that may have slipped between the cracks.

"I assure you we are not looking for information on negotiations or contracts that is within your own security, and we will not discuss or disclose anything you tell us."

John asked: "May I ask what the rumor is that you are looking into is about?"

Linda smiled and answered: "Yes, of course, the rumor is that there is a significant change in the works that may affect international shipping of agricultural products to the far east and, at the same time, reduce the current production from our own Midwest farms."

John sat back in his chair and smiled at Linda and said: "I understand! Well, there are always rumors about shipping changes and negotiations going on, but usually, they are used as a form of the negotiation themselves. However, this time maybe there is something we have all overlooked.

"I believe you said that there could be a decrease in U. S. agricultural production and an increase in Asian production, causing a change in shipping of the products; is that right?"

Linda nodded and said: "In essence, that was the rumor."

John looked thoughtful, and remembering an unusual occurrence, said: "Funny you should bring that up. About a month ago, four of us, all friends from different companies here in lower New York, met for lunch at the Chinese restaurant we all go to every Friday for lunch.

"That day Gene Elbridge, who is a trading broker on the Mercantile exchange, was late arriving. He told us that he had received a last-minute call from an investor in Switzerland who placed a large order to sell two hundred mixed agricultural New York one-year future contracts and, at the same time, buy similar Shanghai future contracts.

"He wasn't able to do the trades at that time, because the Shanghai markets were already closed for the weekend, but on Monday he was able to execute the trades.

"We all discussed it while we ate and wondered why an individual investor would make such an unusual trade. Arbitrage trades like that are usually only done by international banking companies and usually only in precious metals or currencies."

Linda asked: "What would such a trade have to do with shipping contracts?"

John smiled and said: "The transportation and distribution of a product is affected by the availability of the product itself. By selling off the projected future production of a product, it indicates the need for that product is going to shrink. Buying the projected future production has the opposite effect.

"If an investor knows, or thinks he knows, that product production is going to change, and he understands the impact it would cause, he makes such a move as this guy in Switzerland did."

Linda asked: "How would he know what was going to happen?"

John answered: "It requires knowledge of a likely occurrence, in this case, he indicated he had heard something from some scientists that told him there was likely a big change in food production coming. That is all we know.

"All four of us watched the market for a few weeks, and his trade did upset it for a few days, but it has now recovered to near what it had been before."

John sat back and thought for a minute, turned to Linda and said: "Just a minute, I wonder if the news reports about the Chinese nuclear site that they explained to the U.N. last week would have anything to do with this? The scientific communities are all mixed about it, but it did have something to do with food production."

Linda nodded and said: "Yes, I too read about the China nuclear project. Thank you, I did not make that connection, but I now see how it could affect a lot of our country's economy. It could be a hit on many farmers and companies, yours included.

"Please don't misunderstand me I don't for a moment believe that you or your corporation is in anyway involved. However, now that both you and I are aware of the potential, of such an occurrence, we both may share the same intensive concern about it.

"So, may I ask if you have any thoughts about the direction you think we should take in order to determine how much this may affect everything?"

"No, I don't;" answered John, "but now that you have brought it up, I assure you that we are going to look carefully at any and all negotiations that are always on going.

"Our corporate involvement ends at the international ports of import and export, and most negotiations that we have are only with the trucking unions and the agricultural provider and distribution communities.

"The overseas and international shipping, along with all the required import and export compliances, reside with those international shipping companies such as 'Pacific Ocean Shipping Corporation' owned and operated by the billionaire Harvey Wassel."

As Linda rose to leave, she said: "I want to thank you again for your insight and help, the information you have given me definitely helps me move into a field we had not previously considered."

Again, please know that we at NSIU consider this conversation and meeting confidential and we promise we will keep you informed if anything changes. There are, of course, no restrictions upon you or your company, other than to ask that you do not mention our interest unless it is unavoidable."

John, also rising to shake her hand, said: "You may rest assured that we will look carefully into what is happening; for we have well over four thousand employees who work for us, and their future is as important to us as it is to our country.

"Thank you for your contact information and that you now have mine as well, so please feel free to call me or ask me anything that you think can help. I will text you the contact information of the other three friends that were at the lunch with me that Friday.

"I will tell them of our conversation, and I am sure they will be happy to give you their thoughts as well."

Linda said: "Again thank you very much for your cooperation, I assure you we will keep in touch; good bye."

As she left the office and walked down the hall to the elevators, she was thinking he was very helpful and really meant what he had said about his concerns for the agricultural community. She, herself, was the product of a farming lifestyle having grown up on a dairy farm in Vermont; and was concerned about what really could happen with the economy.

She thought she would head back to her office in Washington and look into this China food production idea in a little more detail.

13

Monday, 12 June 2018
NSIU Offices
Washington, D.C.

Linda walked into her office, sat down and began to read over her notes from the meeting in New York. A few minutes later Paul came in, handed her a cup of coffee, and asked if he could run a few thoughts by her.

Both Paul and Linda had found over time, that their brains worked together very well, and often were on the same path to discovery of a subject, but frequently from different directions.

Paul sat down across from Linda, looked into her eyes and said: "Have you and I discussed anything about the NASA satellite photos that were sent to us about three weeks ago?"

Linda answered as she sipped her coffee: "No, I've been floating around up in New York City chasing a rumor and looking to find out if some kind of leaked knowledge regarding unusual financial actions have been going on; you know, insider trading and such. It was about an international rumor that Harold got ahold of, and he wanted me to see if there was anything there.

Paul handed her a copy of the photos from the file and said: "Well, it seems that a satellite took some very detailed photographs as it passed over eastern China, by Suzhou. These photos show a construction site that some of our scientists believed was the beginning of a fusion nuclear site. It got sent over for us to look at, and also to UNAG at the UN.

"The twist is, the Chinese don't deny it, and on the contrary they have gone to long lengths to explain it. Just last week, they sent their own scientist to address the UN General Assembly about it and explain the theory they are building it under."

Linda with that usual smile on her face said: "Here we go again Paul, I've been looking over my notes from a meeting I had just yesterday with a trucking company executive; and the topic we discussed turned to a food production project in China that was being explained the other day at the U.N. General Assembly by the Chinese.

"He, and several of his associates, had discussed a strange international financial trade that was made by an investor from Switzerland about a month ago. It involved the effect of a nuclear action on agricultural production. It apparently was from a tip he received, from some scientist he knew, that there could be a change in the agricultural markets between the United States and China.

"It seems that the Chinese have been promoting the theory that enhanced agricultural production will change the way food distribution in Asia is handled."

Paul set his own coffee down on the corner of Linda's desk and said: "The building of the nuclear facility they are speaking of seems to be the same one the satellite photos show.

"Harold and Jane went up to Germantown to meet and talk with one of our atomic energy specialists, a Dr. Cootes; and he told them he had heard of this theory from a symposium in Hong Kong a couple of years ago. He had actually talked with a Dr. Lee from Shanghai who, I understand, was the Chinese scientific speaker at the Security Council last week."

Linda said: "It would seem that we, once again, are looking at the same situation from different angles. Do you know of any other connections we may have missed?"

"Maybe yes and maybe no." Paul answered: "While we here have been looking into the various reasons for this nuclear facility in China, part of the team, headed by Luigi, had been tasked by the NSA with aiding in the take down of a terrorist cell, and capture of its leader, in Aleppo, Syria.

"The action was successful and once completed, it turned out there was another emergency situation in nearby Lattakia on the Syrian coast.

It seems that another cell had just popped into Turkey and captured five civilian archeologists, one of which was an American.

"Since the team was already still there on the aircraft carrier, the admiral and the DOD, along with the State department, cleared them to attempt an emergency extraction of the civilians from that second cell as well. With good planning, a quick response, and a lot of help from the navy, it too was successful."

Linda said: "I am grateful that those operations were successful, and everything went well, but what does that have to do with our Chinese nuclear plant?"

"I'm getting to that," Paul said: "It seems that the admiral wanted our team to escort the civilians to their home embassies in Greece, so as to assure the countries involved knew that we had had their best interests in mind.

"It turned out that the civilians are international archeologists and are from the USA, the UK, France, Germany, and China. When all the embassy notifications had been made, both the team and the civilian survivors all wanted to celebrate, so together they went to dinner that evening in Athens.

"They got along very well; especially Carl and Lijuan, the girl from China. What makes this even more strange, is the fact that Carl and Lijuan are both very deeply involved with the study of ancient history and, have also developed a strong attachment to each other.

"The attachment is strong enough that, even in only a few short weeks, Carl was moved to talk to the admiral and advise him that, with his current enlistment now almost at its end, it would be best for him not to reenlist in the active navy but remain as an inactive reservist till his term is over. It would let him, therefore, return to teaching history at CTU and not, in any way, compromise the work of our unit.

"Oh! By the way, it turns out that Lijuan is the daughter of Dr. Lin Chang Lee who is the scientific director of the project and is the one who spoke at the UN Security Council."

Linda sat back with surprise and said: "Wow!

"We seem to have a lot of roads leading to China and its nuclear facility. I guess it leads us to ask: Is it good or bad, helpful or harmful, safe or dangerous, economical or expensive?

"Do we have a political problem as well; isn't the White House involved in trade negotiations with China?"

Paul answered: "Yes to the last, negotiations are underway. As for the other points, we don't know. However, I think we need to get very serious about how we approach finding out."

Linda said: "Maybe we need to have a conference with Harold, Jane, the admiral and maybe Luigi and Ira to determine if we have enough to come up with some sort of an action plan, what do you think?"

Paul said: "I agree, there are a lot of variables that individually aren't all that clear. Maybe if we all put our minds to it in open discussion, it may prioritize these items into a workable direction. Should we go talk to the admiral?"

Linda stood up and said: "Let's go!"

About an hour later, they all met in the conference room and went over the various points that Paul and Linda had found. There was agreement that each of these trails came from very different angles, but what did it do to the basic fact that the Chinese nuclear facility was being built and what did it do to America's position?"

It was Harold who said: "I think that we need to reassess exactly what the use of this Chinese nuclear facility is for, and what it really is capable of.

"For example, the only real determination that it will increase food quality or production, as has been explained by a number of international scientists, has always been referred back to the theory that was presented by CERN. We haven't had any corroboration from any other testing source.

"So, with that in mind, for what other useful reason would the Chinese go to the expense of building the facility?"

Jane spoke: "When we talked to Dr. Cootes up at the DOE in Germantown, he said that he also was skeptical, but willing to grant that the project was feasible. When we considered it, there was also the potential as an addition to their electrical grid that was, although somewhat inefficient, a possibility. Looking at the cheap labor available in China, it could be built for about half of what it would cost most western countries to build. It could be a useful source for their grid even if the food idea proved to be 'bogus'."

The admiral looked up and said: "OK, so we give the Chinese an acceptable reason to build the damn thing, what does that have to say about the existing ongoing trade negotiations?"

Linda said: "That was the inference I got from the conversation I had with John Carrick of the Central U. S. Trucking Corporation.

"He told me he had heard about an international agricultural futures trade made by an investor in Switzerland that, in essence, indicated a strong expectation for a significant increase in Asia food production and a similar decrease here in the USA at the same time.

"That would have a large impact on multiple industries; farmers, processors, distributers, trucking, shipping, etc.

"It seems that the tipoff of the potential shift came from some unknown scientists from Europe; and the actual futures trade, although executed, had only a short-term effect on the market."

The admiral said: "None the less, if a wealthy investor is willing to gamble on a theory, perhaps he has other inside knowledge as well. Who, in our country would best be advantaged by a decrease in U.S. agricultural production?"

Paul, having been quiet so far, said: "Assuming that the food production is the primary reason for the site, the overseas shipping companies would be the least affected. They could just change their shipping routes to Asia based routes and continue as they are currently doing."

14

Tuesday, 12 June 2018
Nuclear Fusion Construction Site
Near Suzhou, China

China Defense Secretary Lieu had arrived in Suzhou from Beijing early that morning and met, at the nearby nuclear construction site, with Minister Fu Li Meilin and General Dong Chao Jing who had both arrived the previous day from New York.

The three men were being driven around the site, on an electric cart, to look at how progress had advanced.

Although the facility was established and had been explained as a Tokamak reactor to accelerate food production, the three men paid little attention to the actual building of the large structured Helix that was the heart of the process, or the oval shaped magnetically lined 'Hadron Collider' tunnel that surrounded the huge site.

Their interest was centered on the eight reinforced concrete rooms, each at twenty-five meters square (about eighty-two ft.) and six meters deep (about twenty ft.). They were located near the Northeast end of the large site. Each of these massive below ground rooms were being covered over with a huge arched and reinforced, pre-stressed concrete roof, and all interior surfaces were being covered with a thick lead sheathing.

There was a five-meter-wide (about sixteen ft.), four-meter-high (about thirteen ft.), concrete tunnel connecting the eight rooms with each other and, subsequently, extended over three kilometers (about two miles) underground to a remote ground level truck and train loading area. There were two electric operated and automated load transfer trains that could move massive amounts of materials and items to and from the rooms and the remote loading dock.

There was a one meter thick, lead lined, concrete door that was mounted on tracks at each of the room entrances.

Over this part of the construction site, extensive temporary camouflage netting had been installed to cover as much of the work going on below as possible. This was in an effort to hide and confuse any satellite or aerial photography that may be taken from above. It was planned that this area and the rooms below, when finished, would be completely hidden by trees and fields.

The large oval, magnetically lined tunnel, approximately four kilometers in diameter (about two and one-half miles), that could be seen above ground and surrounded the area above those hidden rooms was a 'Hadron Collider'.

Although it was only a fraction the size of the huge collider tunnel located at CERN in Switzerland, it too was built to be an asset for the educational and experimental study of particle physics by the scientific community in China.

It had been an additional incentive for Beijing to agree to provide the high cost of funding that the project was going to require.

The eight huge hidden rooms below, had a far more sinister intention, and their use and existence were to be kept secret from the outside world.

Even Dr. Lee, although he was the overall project director, did not know the purpose for these rooms; only that they were being built to very specific specifications, and that no one, except specially authorized defense department personnel, was allowed access to the area.

The labor crews working on these rooms were not the same people working on the rest of the project and were kept apart under continuous watch and security.

Dr. Lee had strongly objected to the inclusion of a secret project being built on the site along with his agricultural enhancement project. But he caved when he was told, in no uncertain terms, that it was to be included or his project, and perhaps his own career, would-be dead-on arrival.

The likely scientific probability of providing more and better food production, to the many impoverished people in his own country, was just too strong a cause for him to ignore. That, and he had received a very polite and personal request, from the General Secretary himself, to allow the Defense Secretaries' project to be built on the same site and share in the necessary funding the combination of projects would require.

Dr. Lee, although uncomfortable with the hidden secret area, was honored by the request from the General Secretary and had agreed to progress with the project as described.

As they drove around the secret construction area, Minister Meilin, General Jing and Secretary Lieu used their cart tour to have a private conversation as they looked at the progress that was being made. It was General Jing who briefed the Secretary on the meetings and conversations they had with the representatives from Guatemala, Honduras, Costa Rico, Nicaragua, El Salvador, Columbia, Panama and Venezuela.

He told the Secretary: "They were all interested in the concept of moving their alliance away from Cuba, Russia and Iran. It seems that the promise of a more stable supply of materials, to reduce the pressure they are feeling from their own population, is a very positive one.

"In addition, they have begun to realize that the promised protection being provided by Cuba, in particular, is more verbal than what was actually available. The protection, which was supposed to be provided by Russia and even less from Iran, is subject to much restriction.

"The structure for providing those leaders with support has eroded over time and they have been feeling the pressure from their own populations.

"We don't really know if Venezuela will even be capable of surviving. Their leader has had so far, the military's backing; but the population is growing in anger to the continued loss of prosperity and has been fighting back."

Minister Meilin picked up the narrative, saying: "The real advantage we have is our capacity for uninterrupted shipping.

"They were impressed with the concept of all of the existing shipping ports along the east coast of Asia. With our influence over the Panama

Canal shipping ports, and with both Atlantic and Pacific sea ports in Guatemala, Honduras, Costa Rico, Nicaragua, El Salvador and Columbia, they are beginning to believe that China is a much better ally than they currently have.

"Of course, we are far less restricted by the Americans in our shipping routes; and we are therefore far more capable of providing uninterrupted trade for their products."

General Jing said: "If this happens, as you have planned, we should be able to secure locations to transport and store radioactive materials in those countries and perhaps, eventually even secure complete political control of them."

Secretary Lieu said: "Very good, we are moving ahead in a good direction. I have had several notes from United States shipping magnate Harvey Wessel, and he is on board with changing his fleet operations to accommodate the expected increase in Central America and China's needs.

"The funny part of it is, he believes that the agricultural change, made by the food process change here, is more likely to alter international shipping routes anyway.

He also is going to want security when this all goes down, for he believes he may not be able to remain in the United States if they find out about his involvement in the expected decline of the Midwest agricultural markets."

The overall site construction had been in process over eighteen months and was still about four months short of completion.

The secret rooms had been covered over with dirt, the trees and grasses were being planted and workers were removing the camouflage nets as the area became unrecognizable from the surrounding land.

The Tokomak and the Hadron Collider tunnel were also almost finished, and the detailed scientific startup, verification and validation process was starting.

The support buildings, silos, agricultural process storage warehouses, and the offices along with class rooms were also complete, and the necessary furniture and equipment was being moved in.

Near the western end, the electrical grid transformers were being connected into twelve high voltage wire towers and ready to supply the existing system.

The planned official start date was set for 12 October 2018, so there was much pressure for the validation process to be completed and the project declared ready to produce.

The secret rooms would be ready to begin receiving radio-active materials in about two weeks.

15

Saturday, 16 June 2018
Hilton hotel
Washington, D.C.

It was strange that although Mandarin Chinese was their native tongue, Dr. Lee and his wife had insisted that Lijuan learn English from early childhood, and that it would become her preferred language. With his wealth and position in the Chinese Research Science department, he had been able to send Lijuan to an American Christian Orthodox private school in Shanghai where all her classes were taught in English.

Her teachers, and many of her classmates, all spoke English as their primary language; and although she was completely bilingual, it became more common for Lijuan to communicate in English, she even had an American accent.

Carl, dressed in civilian clothes, was walking over to the Hilton hotel by Union Station. He had received a phone call from Lijuan telling him that she and her father were visiting in Washington and that her father said he would like to meet him. This was the reason Carl had made his decision, so he had asked Admiral Walker for his advice since he was still on active duty.

The admiral had told Carl to take the day off, go and meet Dr. Lee and Lijuan and to be himself. He said that he knew and trusted Carl's integrity and loyalty without reservation, and believed he would assess his relationship with care, and would always make the right decision.

Carl said: "Lijuan asked me if it would be possible for her father to meet with you, sir. She said her father was very thankful for the safe rescue of the archeological group and wanted to personally thank you. I told her I would ask if it is possible."

The admiral sat quietly and just looked at Carl. After a few seconds, he said: "Carl, that places an interesting edge on the discussion. You have not been involved with any operations concerning the Chinese, except of course the rescue of Lijuan; however, we do have some ongoing items that are within our scope of interest.

"I do not wish to put you in any uncomfortable position, so I will answer your request by simply saying that I will check with the state department and follow their advice. You may tell Dr. Lee that you have asked me and that I told you that I will respond directly with him."

Carl walked up and into the hotel entrance and saw Lijuan sitting on one of the lounge chairs in the lobby. She spotted Carl as he entered, could not keep the smile off her face, jumped up and threw herself into his arms.

As Carl caught her, he realized that the hollow feeling, that had been in his chest, began to disappear. He really was glad that this meeting with Lijuan was as warm and loving as it seemed to be.

He had wondered if their first encounter back in Greece was truly as sweet as he had believed it had been. As they stood there and held each other tight, neither of them wanted to let go.

Lijuan, very tall for a Chinese girl at almost five foot ten inches, could look Carl straight into his eyes even though he was six foot one. For several moments they just stared into each other's eyes, and then slowly a sweet lingering kiss just occurred.

As they turned and walked, hand in hand, over toward the coffee shop, an older tall Chinese man stood and watched them as they approached. He was trying to keep a stern look on his face but was not succeeding. He gave it up, and broke into a bright smile as Lijuan introduced Carl to him.

Carl spoke first: "I am very honored to meet you Dr. Lee, please forgive the unsightly greeting that I gave Lijuan, but I must admit that I truly missed her."

Dr. Lee laughed and said: "I like you, you took the blame without hesitation, even when it was Lijuan who threw herself at you and not the other way around." He frowned down at his daughter, who had lowered her head in shame, smiled and said: "Lijuan, go find us a table in the coffee shop and this young man and I will join you in a moment.

As she walked over to the entrance, Dr. Lee said: "Truth be known, she has talked about this meeting with you for weeks now, and I admit I also wished to meet you as well. For two reasons; first, to say thank you for your part in her rescue along with the others, and second because I could see the affection, she has for you specifically, and I wanted to know if it was shared or only her."

Carl standing tall and looking directly into Dr. Lee's eyes, said: "It is shared; from the moment we met, I think we both knew it was to be, and I ask for your permission to proceed with our developing relationship."

Dr. Lee smiled and said: "I don't think I could stop it even if I wanted to, and I don't want to."

The early brunch in the coffee shop was pleasant, and conversation was that of people coming to a new world and seeing the adventures that surrounded them.

Carl told them that he had been given the day off and would be honored to be their guide around the Washington area.

He mentioned that he had spoken to Admiral Walker and was told that the admiral would get in touch with Dr. Lee directly if and when they can meet.

He then told both Dr. Lee and Lijuan that his active duty navy enlistment would be completed in two weeks' time. He told them that he had decided to become a civilian again, and then head back to his home near Austin, Texas.

He explained that he was returning to his previous profession as a history professor at Central Texas University (CTU). He said they seemed happy to have him back, and he would begin teaching classes again the last week of August at the start of the fall semester.

He said: "I believe many of my experiences and world travels, while in the navy, have given me a much more rounded view and understanding of history and the people who lived it, so many years ago."

Lijuan spoke: "I understand what you are saying Carl, for when I was working on the ancient digs in Turkey, it became obvious to me that the people of that time, although with similar personal interests, addressed things in a very different way than we see them today."

Dr. Lee sat back and listened to the two younger people as they discussed their common topic of the study of history, and even their combined future desires to make more discoveries. He smiled to himself knowing that he wouldn't be losing his daughter but would be gaining a brilliant young man who could not hide the love and caring he had for her. He had realized that they truly were meant for each other.

Lijuan, with her master's degree in archeology, coupled with her experiences in Asia and the Middle East, wondered if she could establish an expedition to research some of the ancient Indian tribes that roamed the Southwestern USA; and would it be possible to get a grant from either China or the USA, maybe both.

Carl thought that it might be possible, particularly if CTU was amiable to the idea. Lijuan would however, need to return to China and obtain a working visa in order to do such research in the USA. He didn't think that it would be difficult, and grant funds could probably be obtained.

Lijuan thought she would need to visit several universities, including CTU, to see if it was possible for her to arrange an archeological research project in the west Texas area where the tribes had been two thousand years ago

It would be her teaching position, that she would guide students in the proper procedures for locating, accessing and preserving ancient artifacts, and discovering or determining the appropriate knowledge from them.

Carl thought to himself, he would make some phone calls to the appropriate department heads at CTU and ask them to receive Lijuan and listen to her proposal.

Carl was aware that Dr. Lee had come to America to give a presentation to the United Nations but had not asked him about it. He thought he would be crossing a line he shouldn't cross if he mentioned it, so he resolved not to bring it into the discussion.

The conversation moved to the Lee's home in Shanghai, and they spoke of the modern construction that had dramatically changed the look of the city in only twenty-five years.

Carl told them his only experiences in China had been travel to Hong Kong, Hangzhou and Guangzhou, as part of an escort team for a U.S. Naval Attaché.

Lijuan spoke of her time in Beijing at the university, but she only had an opportunity to travel to very few of the famous ancient sites. Those areas were always kept for archeologists with very strong political influence.

She was interested in the Great Wall and had even walked almost one hundred miles of it, but it was now more of a tourist site rather than a place to study history. Asia history had been well documented for the past two thousand years, so digging up new areas for study required special access and authorization, and it wasn't always available.

After their brunch was finished, they left and began their private guided tour of Washington with Carl showing them most of the more interesting sites.

16

Tuesday evening, 10 July 2018
Tokomak Nuclear Site
Near Suzhou, China

Dr. Lee had spent most of the last two weeks moving his office from Shanghai to his newly finished office building on the site of the new facility near Suzhou. He was comfortable with the new facility, as most of the finishing details from the construction phase had been completed. The view of the very modern looking Helix and Hadron Collider, that was surrounded by traditional trees and beautiful landscaping, was enough to put one's mind at ease.

The start up procedures and the validation of all the components had begun, but it would be several months before the real tests could happen. Until the actual conversion of the agricultural protein was performed and confirmed, it was still an expensive gamble and the risk was firmly on Dr. Lee's shoulders.

He had been very busy interviewing a number of scientists, they would be the operating professionals of the procedures and provide the quality control necessary. It wasn't easy to find them, for the process had still not been proven and there was a question in everyone's mind if it was going to work.

There were four separate components of the project with the agricultural the most widely known, but the electrical grid portion was also there, and the educational studies portion needed to be verified as well. It was the underground security sector that was unknown to the rest of the people on site, and that worried Dr. Lee a lot.

He did not know what the intention was, and therefore could not assess if it would conflict with the other areas. As director of the entire project, he could not shake the feeling that the area hidden from him was not only dangerous, but also a violation of an international agreement. However, all his requests for information went unanswered.

There were reports of guarded trains and trucks coming and going to the remote loading and unloading facility several kilometers away, but security was tight at that location and no one spoke of it.

He was sitting at his desk with a pile of validation reports that he needed to sign off on, when a younger female scientist, who was a nuclear physicist, knocked on his door and asked to see him. She had been doing studies of possible radioactive contamination, within the Helix, and had gotten a strange unusual reading from an area outside that should never have been there.

She gave him a report from several sample dosimeter locations, located around the site, that showed a level of radioactivity that was higher than would normally or reasonably be found. What was so unusual, was the system had not yet been fueled or started, so where had the source of contamination come from?

If they were getting readings like this now, what could they expect when the system was up and running?

Dr. Lee was angry! Enough was enough!

He did not know what was in the secure area, but the readings were obviously from high intensity contamination materials, and they were leaking out into the atmosphere.

He picked up his telephone and called Defense Secretary Lieu; and, after being told that he was unavailable, hung up and called the General Secretary's office and asked for an opportunity to meet with him in Beijing. He knew that he would be stepping on some high political toes, but the safety and performance of his project had to be put before such things.

His meeting with the General Secretary, the following week, was short and rather disappointing. Defense Secretary Lieu was present and kept stepping in on the report Dr. Lee was presenting with regard to the measured radioactive levels that had appeared; saying that they were aware of the contamination readings and that they were well below acceptable levels.

Dr. Lee said that the unknown source of radioactive contamination could well have an adverse effect on the agricultural procedure. Secretary Lieu said his experts had reviewed it and had assured that it would have no such effect.

Quietly Dr. Lee, looking at the two men seated across from him, realized in that moment that it had all been a set-up; for it was he and his staff who were the most highly qualified experts in all of China, so just who were Secretary Lieu's experts.

Dr. Lee sat quietly and listened to the conversation between the Defense Secretary and the General Secretary, and realized, although they didn't say so, they would not change anything at this point; but he also realized that his career was coming to an end.

He hoped that they would, at least, let him prove the food enhancement portion of the project before replacing him. However, he began to think he would need to plan for whatever the future may hold.

As he rode on the train back to Suzhou, he let his thoughts drift back to the time he and Lijuan were with Carl in Washington. He felt pleased that his daughter was in such a good relationship and was comfortable that she would be protected.

Admiral Walker had called and invited him to meet at an area restaurant while he was still in Washington. It had been a pleasant dinner, and Lieutenant Jarred and Lieutenant JG McCalla, all dressed in civilian clothes were with them. The admiral had said that they were very interested in the food protein project and had asked if they could come along to ask him about it.

It had been a very pleasant dinner, and they all talked about the rescue and the events leading up to it. He had thanked the admiral for so quickly deciding to provide a rescue mission that would save so many from different countries, including his only daughter.

Discussion of the Tokomak project was mostly a repeat of the presentation he had given at the UN, but Harold and Jane took the opportunity to ask questions about the cost vs. production ratio that had so bothered them. Dr. Lee had said he also was concerned, but with the scientific studies available and the additional electrical power grid supply that would also happen, there was a more productive outlook.

He smiled to himself as he road along on the train. They had not pressured him, although he was sure they knew far more about the project than they had said, he knew that they hadn't gained anything new from him.

Now, after his meeting in Beijing, he wasn't even sure that he would be allowed to complete the project, and thus was grateful that Lijuan had been cleared with her work visa. She was now back in America meeting with several universities, in Texas and Arizona, trying to gain funding or grants for her archeological project.

While he was riding along, he placed a short cell phone call to Carl in Austin and asked him, without explaining why, if he could please try to keep her in America, and not let her come back to China.

When the train arrived at the station, on the west end of Suzhou, he walked to the parking lot for his car. He noticed that there were two plain clothed security guards that followed him. They were still behind him when he got to his new apartment. He was not a fool, he knew that they had been assigned to shadow him and report his movements back to Beijing. He was glad he had called Carl from the train, they would not have had enough time to set up a trace on his cell phone that fast.

17

Tuesday, 10 July 2018
Central Texas University
Faculty Housing Center
Austin, Texas

Carl had been up and already had his morning coffee when the cell phone call came through from Dr. Lee.

He had requested that Carl try and keep Lijuan in America and not let her go back to China. He didn't explain why, and Carl, having been an experienced investigator, knew that it was not the time to ask.

Carl said that he would keep her busy and safe while she was here, and for her father not to worry. He added that he would be available if and when he was needed.

Lijuan had been off in Arizona for the past three days and was not scheduled back until the coming weekend. Carl thought she didn't need to know about the call just yet, and he would just keep her busy until he could get some answers.

He didn't know what was happening, but he did know who to advise about it. With the time change, the staff at NSIU would all be in, so he put through a call to Washington. It was Paul DeNice who was the first one to answer.

Paul said he was happy to hear from him and asked how civilian life was treating him. Carl said: "Paul, I am calling because I just got a very strange telephone call from Lijuan's father. It was a very short call, and he simply asked that if I could please make sure Lijuan stays in America and does not return to China."

Paul said: "Hold on Carl, do you still have your satellite phone?"

Carl answered: "I still have it and, as per instructions, will for the next two years while I am on reserve status."

Paul said: "Call back on it using 119F code."

Carl said: "Understood, five minutes."

He walked into the bedroom and opened his lock safe an drew out his navy issued satellite phone, put on his shoes and socks and walked out of the house and across to the open park across the street. Now, with no one around, he called Paul's satellite phone and when it was answered, took the letter 'F', as the sixth letter of the alphabet, and added it to the 119-code number, he simply said encode 125 and entered it on his own keypad.

Paul said laughing: "I see you haven't forgotten the voice code alteration. Hang on, the admiral wants to listen to this."

Admiral Walker spoke up and said, "hello Carl, what is this phone call from Dr. Lee?"

Carl answered: "Good morning sir, I got a very strange telephone call from Dr. Lee early this morning. He said that he wanted me to make sure that Lijuan did not leave America and not to let her travel back to China.

"Although I don't know her father well, I believe he is truly a good man and is worried that Lijuan could be in danger if she goes back to China. That makes me believe he is also in danger and that, with his position in the government, he is worried about his own future and Lijuan's."

Admiral Walker said: "How much do you know about Dr. Lee's project in Suzhou?"

Carl answered: "Only what has been in print and what was said at the United Nations. Our conversation while he was here, was mostly centered around the relationship between Lijuan and me."

Admiral Walker said: "Very well Carl, although you aren't on active duty any longer, I would ask that you please keep us informed of anything further that you hear."

Carl answered: "Absolutely sir! Lijuan is very important to me, but so is the duty I swore to more than four years ago, and although a reservist, I am still in the navy.

"I will of course let you know if anything changes, but I wanted to mention that I feel Dr. Lee could be in an uncomfortable position, and I may need help keeping Lijuan here once she learns her father may be in trouble."

Admiral Walker said: "We will watch out for her as well, and you will know what we can let you know as our investigation moves along. Good luck Carl!"

Carl sat and watched the little 'E' on his phone screen blink out. He wondered exactly what had happened to drive Lijuan's father to make such a phone call. He had called on an unsecure cell phone but said very little. However, his asking that Carl keep Lijuan from traveling to China, was a strong indication something was very wrong.

Lijuan is, and had always been, a Chinese citizen, and with her father as a part of the Chinese government, albeit in the scientific community, it was very strange that he would be afraid of her coming back there. Such a situation could really only mean that he himself was in a dangerous position.

Carl resolved not to tell Lijuan about the call from her father unless and until it became absolutely necessary.

Back in Washington, Paul and the admiral sat and looked at each other. It was the admiral who spoke first: "What could have happened that would drive such a brilliant man to be so worried that he didn't want his daughter to come home to her native country?"

Paul just shook his head and said: "I have no idea sir, but the fact is he did just that."

The admiral said: "Paul, put in a request for any information that may have slipped by our door and landed at the CIA. Maybe they have a smidgen of information that they aren't following that may help explain what we now know.

"Also, ask Lieutenant Jarrett if maybe he would go back up to the DOE and ask that nuclear scientist he talked to if he has any ideas. Tell him to ask if he can think of anything that would frighten someone, as brilliant as Dr. Lee, enough to want to prevent his only child from returning to China."

Paul said: "Aye sir, I'll get right on it."

He went in search of Harold Jarrett and found him in the coffee room talking to Jane McCalla. He asked if he could interrupt for a moment, was told yes, and he began to describe the morning's event starting with the phone call from Carl.

He asked: "So, the question is sir, ma'am, what would frighten such a man as Dr. Lee to the point of asking that we keep his daughter in the USA and not let her return to China?"

It was Jane who said: "I wonder if something happened at the new site that was unexpected and was in danger of exposing something sinister going on there. We have photos that were taken from the international space station recently, but they only show the Tokomak and the Hadron Collider along with their support buildings and offices. But we have not seen or heard of anything regarding fuel tests yet."

Paul said: "The admiral asked me to ask if you could go back up the DOE, and maybe ask that scientist you met if he has any thoughts as to what would scare Dr. Lee so much."

Harold said: "I'll call and go up there this afternoon, if he is available."

Jane spoke up: "I have a meeting with congress woman Sally Martin this morning, but after lunch, I can go over to the CIA and poke through their correspondence regarding that project and see if anything turns up."

Paul said: "Thank you for volunteering, I was about to ask if you had any suggestions also."

"While you are there, could you maybe try to find out if we have any assets in Suzhou?"

Jane answered: "I'll see what I can find out."

18

Wednesday, 11 July 2018
Ivan Nub's Restaurant
NYC

Linda had received a telephone call yesterday from John Carrick at Central U.S. Trucking Corporation. He was inviting her to come to a meeting scheduled on Wednesday at his office. He told her that she could meet and talk to the others who had been at the Chinese luncheon two months ago.

The international shipping component was something she had thought about but, with the exception of the discussion she had with Paul, little else was known. She hadn't found anything that would upset the current investigation into the nuclear aspect of the China site; but something about the concept bothered her a lot.

As she walked into the offices of Central U. S. Trucking Corporation at 11:30 in the morning, John Carrick was already waiting for her in the lobby. He rose from the very soft chair he was in and with a big smile said: "Good morning Ms. DeSanto, I am so glad you could come meet with us today."

Linda, quite surprised at the warm welcome from a corporate director, said: "Thank you, I am pleased you called, please call me Linda."

John smiled and said: "I am meeting you down here today because my associates decided they wanted to relax and meet with you, and the best way to do that was at lunch.

"So, they played 'Rock-Paper-Scissors" to see who would buy, and although there were four of us and we were all on a conference call and could not verify the winner, I was told that unfortunately I lost.

"It is of course my pleasure, and please know I will get even with them at the first chance I get."

Linda said: "It sounds as if you four people are not only business associates, but very good friends as well."

"Very true," he said as they got into a taxi: "But we all have different views of the financial and business world.

"Also, be prepared, they are very nosy and will probably pester you until they know everything about you. However, they are all very good people, and very discrete or they would not have survived this long in the Wall Street Jungle."

When they arrived at Ivan Nub's Restaurant ten minutes later, it was to find that the others were already there and waiting for them in the entrance lobby.

John greeted them with a smile and introduced Linda to them: "Linda, this is Emilio Watson from the International Ocean Shipping Company, Annie Selene of World View Bank International, and Gene Elbridge a futures Trader-Broker on the N.Y. Mercantile Exchange. Folks this is Linda DeSanto from the U.S. Navy Security Investigation Unit in Washington."

After being seated at a round table off to one side of the very high-class restaurant, and placing their orders, light friendly conversation broke out amongst the four friends.

Linda sat and listened to the light banter, realizing that they were just lowering the atmosphere so that she would feel comfortable in the setting. It was a tactic used by many executives when they both wanted someone they didn't know to relax, and maybe be a little more forthcoming with their thoughts.

Annie said: "Linda, please forgive my curiosity, but how did you, a civilian, wind up working directly for the U. S. Navy?"

Linda smiled, thinking that didn't take long, and answered: "I guess you should know a bit about me, I actually was a Sargent in the Vermont State Police.

"A few months ago, I was assigned to a murder investigation in Vermont that had some political and international complications. Because of those features, and along with some other coincidental events, the NSIU got involved. Quite simply, I became the communication coordinator between the state and federal authorities.

"When the case was solved, the admiral in charge of the NSIU, offered me a position as a civilian contract investigator working directly for them. Really, it was an honor and just too good an opportunity to pass up."

Emilio asked: "So what brings you to us, other than a wonderful opportunity to stick John with a really good lunch bill?"

They all laughed, and Linda replied: "I really didn't know that lunch was to be involved; however, I learned many years ago not to look a gift horse in the mouth.

Actually, I had been assigned to look into an action that might have been involved with some international trades; and the possibility of it having some influence on international shipping."

Gene said: "Please forgive us for these questions, but John has told us of the visit you had with him and the possible interest in agricultural production gains and losses that may affect our Midwest economy."

Emilio said: "To be sure you know that our interest is uncompromised, we are aware of the Chinese food production experiment that was explained at the UN a few weeks ago, and of the impact it may have on our own agricultural production. Much of this information has caused us to pause and reflect upon current market movement.

"However, as I understand what John has told you, we knew only of the unusual arbitrage trade that took place in the beginning of May."

Gene told her: "John said he told you of the trades, do you have any question about them I can help you with?"

Linda answered: "I think I understand them, although I admit I had to do some research into that type of futures trading in the international markets. However, isn't it usually a result of some news item or such; and doesn't it usually cause a significant change in the current market?"

Gene said: "Correct on both items. However, all we knew was that the investor from Switzerland said he had some scientist give him a hint that something was likely to happen."

Annie said: "We all watched the international monetary values, and the completed action really didn't change anything very much. We had all thought that was a little strange, until the news reports about a speech at the UN a few weeks ago, given by a Dr. Lee from China, explained their nuclear food enhancement process. He said, however, although they had strong belief that it was true, it was still unproven.

"That did give us pause, but all we have been able to find is what has been in the news. So, yes, we did want to see if anything you can tell us changes our view of what is happening."

Linda said: "I believe that you probably have a better feel of what is going on in that area than I would, but it is a fair question and I wish I had a good answer for you. All I can tell you is that we knew of the project for some time now, and have the same questions about its viability as you have. Even many of our own scientists are unsure of the veracity of the atomic enhancement claim."

Emilio said: "Well, maybe there is something that is happening that may have meaning. John and I are actually involved in the transfer of agricultural products, albeit his company is land based, and mine is primarily ocean shipping.

"So far not much has changed in the past few months, but last week my company's primary competitor, Trans World Shipping Corporation (TWSC), announced that its agricultural export capacity was going to be reduced by about 30% beginning October 2018. There was no explanation given, but TWSC's owner is billionaire Harvey Wassel and he does not usually broadcast his intensions.

"Our reaction is positive because we are his primary competitor and, as long as the international agricultural market remains strong, such an action is good for us. We would be in a position to pick up that portion of the market he is cutting."

John said: "Why we asked you to visit with us today is twofold; one, we want to know if there is a known pending potential, in our industry, that forecasts a loss in a productive market. And two, we felt that your investigation should know, or at least be aware, that a major Ocean shipping company is cutting his U.S. market; and as we found out, is moving a large portion to his China based marketplace."

Linda sat quietly and looked around the table. She didn't know these people well; but had the feeling that they really were concerned about the market place. That was the reason that had prompted the meeting and, was as much for the country's good as it was for their own business's bottom line.

It was obvious that Emilio and John would feel any significant changes immediately, while any change in the economic market would affect the international marketplace as well.

Linda asked: "If I understand what you have said, your concern is; why has Harvey Wassel made such a major change to his business, when it actually benefits your businesses at this time.

It was John that answered: "Well yes, I guess that is what we are saying. Wassel isn't the kind of man who makes sudden changes in his very lucrative business operations. So, the question is what has he learned that we haven't?"

"We know that he has direct ties with the Chinese for international import and export of many products, but his routes had never before included routes to and from China and Central America.

"We pretty much know who and what is going to and from most ports of entry on the Pacific rim, and the Central America trade was always just small time; largely tramp shipping companies out of India and southern Asia.

"Most of those ocean shipping lanes pass through or near Mexican territorial waters, and are, thus, usually monitored by them."

Emilio said: "We have heard that Wassel had several meetings or contact with officials from the Chinese communist party, when they were here a while ago for the Security Council explanation.

"It was only a week later that he made the announcement of his cut back of the US and China shipping routes."

Linda said: "I didn't know about that, thank you. But isn't it a bit strange that there should be a change in shipping to Central American countries that would mean an increase in imports from China?

"What are they importing?

Aren't most of those countries in financial trouble with their economies?"

It was Annie who answered: "Their banking structure isn't too good, and they are largely beholding to Cuba and Russia for their security. That usually causes a decline in imported goods, including food products.

"As a result, much of the societies in those countries rely on illegal drug trafficking to the U.S.A. Perhaps that is the intent of their imports from China, but that already exists."

Emilio said: "If he is dealing with China on their projected food increases, he is risking a lot on the unknown, and that's not like him!"

The conversation continued as their luncheon proceeded, and Linda's thoughts were about trying to figure out why such a change in the shipping business had everyone wondering. She knew she was going to dig into this when she got back to Washington.

19

Monday, 6 August 2018
Tokomak Nuclear Site
Near Suzhou, China

Defense Secretary Lieu had placed a call to Minister Fu Li Meilin, at his remote office in downtown Suzhou, to talk to him about the radioactive levels at the Tokomak site. He said that he had to do some fast covering, with the General Secretary, when Dr. Lee had found that unexplained levels had appeared before they had even begun to fuel the fusion reactor.

Minister Meilin explained that one of the cases had fallen off the transfer train and the top had come loose. They had been able to repair it, but the leak had occurred in the tunnel and not in one of the rooms.

General Dong Chao Jing stepped into the room as Meilin was being dressed down by Secretary Lieu. He hid a small smile, as he turned his head away to hide his pleasure at the minister's discomfort. It had, after all, been Meilin who had promoted the placing of the hidden nuclear waste factory on the site of Dr. Lee's Tokomak fusion food project.

The idea had been to provide an accessible location, where a quantity of dirty bomb weapons could be assembled, packaged and stored. That way, they could be placed in third world countries throughout Central and South America and also within Southern Asia.

These low-level nuclear weapons would provide those third world countries with a strong international negotiating power in exchange for China's promise of support. It would also provide force to increase their personal strength over their own populations.

The added effect would be that China, would be the one to gain a defensive control position over these smaller and very gullible countries, pulling it away from Cuba and Russia in Central and South America and from Iran, Syria and Russia in the Southern Asia areas.

Once the major countries of the western world realized that each of these small third world countries were obtaining a viable nuclear capacity, they would have to spend a tremendous amount of resources and effort in determining how they got there, and, at the same time, apply the necessary pressure and security to disarm them.

As long as the United Nations members were in doubt as to where these countries had obtained those weapons, the Chinese communist ruling party would be in a situation of plausible deniability, as there would be a strong push to have the Atomic Energy Commission (AEC) contain and control their potential use.

A large part of the plan was to provide an acceptable cover for the controlled distribution of these weapons, and that is where Harvey Wassel and his ocean shipping fleet would come into play.

It was Dr. Lee who was the face of the Tokomak food enhancement project, for it was he who had gone to the U.N. with the detailed explanation and its potential; and it was he who was the site project director. When the Chinese involvement in a nuclear dirty bomb weapons plan was exposed, as it most surely would, it would be Dr. Lee who would be blamed.

Although Dr. Lee was completely unaware of the weapons plan, his push for the food enhancement program and its associated international distribution potential, was just the cover that was needed for Secretary Lieu. He knew that they could use it to hide the weapons and get them into those small countries; and Harvey Wassel, a rather ruthless U.S. businessman, with no loyalty other than to building his fortune even greater, was the perfect choice.

Secretary Lieu had put General Jing in charge of manufacturing the dirty bomb weapons; and it was Jing who insisted that they all be completely assembled and secured before any were shipped out. As they were completed, he had them moved into the seven remaining rooms and they were placed in secure containers, labeled in English, and placed in large lead lined cases.

General Jing and Secretary Lieu had agreed that they would not ship any of these weapons until the food enhancement project was in production. If the schedule was correct, that would mean they would be shipping the first containers about the beginning of December.

After his phone call to Meilin, Secretary Lieu sat back in his chair and thought about the meeting he had with the General Secretary and Dr. Lee. He had covered it as well as he could, but he realized that when he told the General Secretary that he had his own experts tell him that there was no problem, that Dr. Lee just looked at him and said nothing. It was a mistake, for Dr. Lee himself, was the most qualified expert in all of China, and it was he who had brought it up.

Right after the meeting, he had sent a security team to follow Dr. Lee and report back to him. There hadn't been much time to set it up, and they really were only able to catch up to him as he got off the train back in Suzhou. However, he was now under a twenty-four-hour watch and had taps on all his communications. They, however, did not know about the cell phone call to Carl in Texas while he was on the train.

20

Monday, 20 August 2018
NSIU Headquarters
Washington, D.C.

Admiral Walker sat at his desk and slowly looked through the six current project files that had been assigned to his unit. He soon realized that, although they had all been assigned to various members of his staff, and were being handled efficiently and properly, he could not get his mind to focus on any of them without drifting off to the China nuclear project.

It was that phone call from Carl that had him wondering what was going on.

The dinner meeting that he, Jane and Harold had with Dr. Lee was both pleasant and innocuous. They had not pressured him in any way, and he had been very forthcoming with his scientific belief that the project was going to help the world with its food supply. There had not been any uncomfortable moments; and as they left him, it was with the feeling that he was indeed a brilliant and fine man.

They had spoken about the romance that was developing between Lijuan and Carl and had all agreed that it would not create any political problems. Both of them were out of any political discussion and deeply involved with the study of ancient history, teaching and each other.

But it had been Lijuan's father who had called Carl to ask him to keep her from returning to China and keep her in America; by all known reason, that was a very strange request. What could have happened that such a man would make that kind of request?

He picked up the rather thick file of investigation reports, and starting with the most recent one, began to read. It was the report from the four friends that Linda had met for lunch and had filed five weeks previously.

It was the part of her report that involved Harvey Wassel that interested him the most.

It said that Wassel has direct ties with the Chinese for their international import and export of agricultural products as well as other container items.

Those routes were for ocean shipping to and from the USA and China. He had however, never before included routes to and from China and Central America; but that was about to change. It further spoke of a significant reduction of shipping from the USA, and an increase from China.

The admiral thought that it was quite a gamble for Wassel to be taking. That wouldn't be a move a successful billionaire would take if he was only banking on the Chinese increasing food production. So, what else did he know that we don't?

Again, the question of why Dr. Lee had asked Carl to keep Lijuan in America kept coming back. It was, after all, a request from a powerful man, in another country, that involved the security of his only daughter.

Having met with Dr. Lee, he just didn't think the doctor was the type of man to make such a request without explanation; unless, a situation was developing that would put him in danger and subsequently, his daughter as well.

It was obvious that he wanted to protect Lijuan from harm and knew that she would be safe in the USA.

He sat forward and picked up his phone and called Harold. He asked him to set up a meeting with Jane, Linda, Paul, and Luigi.

Several hours later, as they all met in the conference room, on the third floor, he began to explain his questions: "I just cannot get past the feeling that we are looking at something we haven't seen before, and I don't mean Food production.

"When we met with Dr. Lee, there was no indication that he knew of anything more than his atomic food production project that he so strongly believes in. All the information we have, regarding the project, is a confirmation of that belief.

"So, the question we need to resolve is; what happened that made him place a call to Carl and to ask him to assure her safety by keeping her in America?"

Jane said: "I checked with the CIA and asked if there was anything that they knew that wasn't in the file, or if we had an asset in or near Suzhou. They said no, they didn't have an asset, and that they didn't know anything more than we did."

Paul said: "Linda and I have talked about the impact of this project and what it could mean to our economy, and there are several issues that just don't make too much sense."

Linda said: "Our sources in New York are all wondering what the economical impact is going to be. There have been several indications that show a potential for a significant reduction in the United States' agricultural production. That was reinforced by the Chinese presentation of their nuclear protein enhancement project in Suzhou. However, with the exception of TWSC, owned by Harvey Wassel, there has been very little impact on any of the markets."

The admiral spoke up: "Linda, as I was reading through your report, you mentioned that Wassel is going to reduce his shipping capacity from the United States to China by about thirty percent in October; also, he apparently is going to begin more direct routes from China to Central and South America, is that correct?"

Linda replied: "That is what they told me, and I am sure they know because Wassel had announced it."

Harold asked: "I wonder why he would be opening up routes to and from China and those countries?" Food production has never been a big problem there, and most of those countries already have adequate product access from the USA and many other countries throughout the Pacific Rim."

Luigi, who had been sitting quietly listening to everyone, looked up and said: "You know, maybe I am just too used to nefarious plots, but aren't a number of these Central and South American countries under the control of poorly run socialist governments?

"Also, I believe that many of them rely on their security from communist controlled Cuba, Russia and, to a lesser extent even Iran. So, why would China be involved with a major shipping change to these countries?"

Admiral Walker looked over at Luigi and said: "Those are good questions, does anyone have any thoughts about that?"

Harold said: "We have known that much of the drug traffic and unregulated Chinese made products have been illegally smuggled into the USA through those countries and Mexico for years. However, there is currently a significant effort, by both us and Mexico, to curb those actions."

The admiral said: "Yes, our agreement with Mexico allows for them to monitor the international ocean shipping lanes to and from those small Central American countries. They have been recently doing increased interdiction that permits them to board and search for illegal drugs."

Harold again spoke up and said: "With the strong policies being pushed by the White House, everyone knows that the US/Mexican border smuggling is headed for a decline. So, I repeat Luigi's question; why would China be involved with a major shipping change to these countries?"

Paul said: "The only connection we have with all of this goes back to the Tokomak project in Suzhou. But it was Dr. Lee, that explained and defended the project at the UN, and it was the same Dr. Lee who has effectively asked us to protect his daughter. So, what has he found out that he is so uncomfortable about?

Looking over at Harold, he asked: "The project over there has been under construction for almost two years now, do we have any source or access to aerial photos of the construction site that we haven't seen?

Harold answered: "I suppose it is possible, the original discovery was from a satellite that no longer exists, maybe it has been replaced and no one thought to tell us about it."

The admiral said: "OK, I think we are all on the same page about this. We don't know what or if anything additional may be happening with the Suzhou project, yet everything seems to revolve around it.

"So, let's get going on finding out. As of now all of us are to look only at this problem and let the other problems and projects be handled by the rest of the staff.

"Start by seeing if we can find a reason for the Chinese to be changing shipping routes, and let's see if we can find out what has scared Dr. Lee enough to want us to protect his daughter. Harold, please be the records coordinator, and Paul, follow up and see if we have any additional reconnaissance available. Let's go and find some answers!"

21

Tuesday, 21 August 2018
NASA Johnson Space Center
Houston, TX

Paul had thought there must have been something that happened at the Suzhou site that has disturbed Dr. Lee quite a bit. From his reaction, it might have been something that could compromise his agricultural program, and he must have stepped on someone's toes when he questioned it.

Paul went over to Jane's office, knocked on her door and asked if he could talk to her and run some ideas by her.

She answered: "Of course Paul, I was trying to think of a move we might have missed; have you come up with something?"

Paul sat down and said: "Maybe. I was thinking, that the size of the site is quite large, but most of the land distance used is because of the magnetic tunnel for the Hadron Collider that runs around the perimeter. That leaves a lot of undisturbed space in the middle of the site. Also, do we actually know what the support buildings are being used for?"

Jane looked at Paul and said: "You have a plan, I can tell, what is it?"

Paul smiled and said: "I think it might be a good idea to go down to NASA Johnson Space Center and see if they have been taking some pictures that nobody thought were unusual. Also, I think maybe it should be both you and me that does the looking."

Jane raised her eyebrows and said: "You think I would see something different than you would?"

Paul answered: "No, but you and I have a different perspective on some things and, as a result, find things that may be important to one idea and be missed by another. You know, 'The Forest for the Trees'."

Jane said: "You have a point. I'll set it up to get us a flight down to Huston tomorrow morning if you can get us to the right place once we are there."

Down in Huston at NASA, Katie Burns was looking at the latest aerial photographs that had been taken over the city of Suzhou from two different sources. One picture was from the international space station and had been manually taken by an American Astronaut; and the other was from a secret spy satellite that had been rerouted to replace the old OPLS just three days after it crashed into the sea.

This new satellite was much faster than the original OPLS, and it was placed in a much narrower trajectory; so, it would pass over a specific site about every seventy-two hours.

To be fair, it was her job to study the many photographs that were tagged for observation by the NSA or the DOD for specific movement of equipment or weapons.

So, as a result, she and most of the other technicians would usually look at the other photos, but without a specific thing to look for, just file them.

It was Katie who had first found the Suzhou site, and it was she who met Jane and Paul, Wednesday morning, at the research center library where the records and photos were kept.

She had been surprised to get the call from Paul yesterday, and had wondered what could have happened.

After the introductions, Jane said with a big smile: "I believe it was your very sharp eyes that first found the construction site in Suzhou that started the chain of events that brings us here today."

Katie answered: "Thank you, I looked back into the files from that day and remembered that I didn't know what they were building."

Paul smiled and said: "Well, it did start up a bit of a fury, and that still goes on. Why we are here today however, is to see if we can find something unusual that may show up on one or more of the many photos that have been taken since then."

Katie took them over to several large screen high definition computer monitors. She then began to explain how they could bring up all the available photos that had been taken of the site.

She showed them that they each could access the same photo at the same time by simply entering the Longitude and latitude of the site, then follow the sequence.

The three of them together began to study the photos, starting with the infamous photo from the OPLS in May, and proceeding to those taken in the following few months.

Paul had been correct in asking Jane to come along today, because about four and a half hours later, it was she who found something that was out of the normal procedure at the construction site.

Jane said: "Paul, I think I found something out of place. Starting from the beginning, the center of the site has just been a vacant, uninteresting landscape with no trees or anything interesting. But if you'll notice the sequence of photos are about three days apart.

"If you pull up the photo from 12 June and compare it with the one from 15 June it appears that the uninteresting vacant area has suddenly become a finished park like landscape including quite a few trees. That is amazing in only three days."

Katie said: "Wow, I never would have picked that up, the colors are so similar, and they just blend in to the photo of the site."

Paul said: "The change was obviously planned, and, of course, they would have known that we were using aerial satellite photography. That way the area would have been kept under camouflage netting, mounted on tall poles, to hide whatever they were building underground."

Jane said: "It would have taken an awful lot of netting; and it would take a great deal of manpower and equipment to remove it in just three days. It must have been done at night as well, so it couldn't be noticed during daylight. They couldn't know the schedule of the satellite, could they?"

Katie shook her head answered: "Unfortunately, they probably could; we know most of theirs and Russia's as well. Computers can predict them pretty accurately these days."

Paul stood up, looked at Katie and Jane and said: "The question now is, what did they build or do under that netting that we don't know about?"

Katie had those photos printed and gave them to Jane who asked: "Now that we all see what we have discovered, could you please let us know of anything you see that is at all weird happening around that park like area?

Katie said: "This is an enlightening experience for me, I have always looked for items that look like weapons or unusual equipment movement. I think, that with this example, I will have all our technicians begin to question any change they see in subsequent photos."

Jane said: "Don't go overboard, we had a specific reason to look at this area and, we didn't know what we were looking for. We still don't, but at least we now know something happened there or why would they have hidden it?"

22

Tuesday, 28 August 2018
Trans World Shipping Company
Home Offices
San Francisco, CA.

Wayne Hon, after having been asked by Harvey Wassel to come to his office for special instructions, was both surprised and honored by the assignment he received from his boss.

Wassel said: "Wayne, I want you to personally manage the acquisition and modifications of three ships for me. These are special ships and I don't want our regular fleet operations people to know anything about them."

He handed Hon a thick file of specifications and a set of prints. He said: "These are the requirements that will need to be included, and make sure you keep this information away from our normal build sources.

"They are to be built in Liberia and we will set up registration from there as well."

Hon, after taking the plans and specifications from his boss, laid them on the conference table and spread them out. He took a quick look at the drawings and, with great surprise, just stared up at him; the documents had been drawn and printed in Chinese.

Hon said: "Sir, you said to have these built in Liberia, their language is English. How do you expect to have these plans understood by the builders?"

Wassel answered: "That is one of the main reasons I wanted you to manage the project. You will not only be necessary for translation, but also to oversee the actual compliance.

"These drawings were prepared by ship designers in China, under the direction of secretary Lieu, and have had very special compartments built into the storage areas."

Hon said: "But sir, as soon as we contract the build, everyone will know that TWSC is doing this and questions will be all over the place."

Wassel smiled and said: "I know, that is why it won't be built by TWSC."

The shocking look in Hon's eyes was one of disbelief. Wassel, with an unusual amount of humor in his eyes, said: "The ships will be owned and modified by the W.H. Shipping Company, of Hong Kong. The W.H. stands for Wayne Hon."

Wayne Hon couldn't help it, his knees just gave out and he fell back, fortunately landing in a chair.

Wassel, who was never one to show any kind of emotion, burst out laughing and said: "The look on your face is astounding.

"Anyway, as you so accurately pointed out, TWSC can't be the direct owner. So, we needed to set up a shell company that would not be looked at too closely. I thought that putting it in Hong Kong would not raise any eyebrows, and we are only modifying three small 'Handy' size ships."

He continued: "I have taken the liberty of using your initials for the company's name, and I have had a Hong Kong legal team working on this for more than three months. I want you to follow up on the ship building portion of this ASAP."

Hon, recovering from the shock, said: "Sir, I am not in a position to take such a gamble with the various government agencies; I am only an employee of TWSC."

Wassel said: "I would not put such a load on you without making sure you are well compensated and well protected from such actions.

"W.H. Shipping Co. has been established, is located in Hong Kong and, as a Hong Kong company, falls under Chinese authority and regulations, not American.

"The funding of the company has been provided by Wassel foundation funds from Saudi Arabia and has a current bank account of seventy-five million dollars.

"You, as the Chief Operating Officer, will receive an annual salary of one million dollars. In addition, you will receive an acceptance bonus of three million dollars.

"Go to your office and think about it, study the plans; and you may speak to the Lawyer in Hong Kong, whose contact information is here as well. I will need your acceptance or decline by this evening."

Wayne Hon was born in Hong Kong. He was a Hong Kong citizen, albeit under British control, until the lease ran out in 1997 and possession of Hong Kong and the Kowloon Peninsula was returned to Mainland China.

The unusual agreement, between China and Hong Kong, allowed for the Hong Kong citizens to retain a British Passport and acknowledged their Hong Kong citizenship. Although it has slowly been changing, most of those unusual rules still applied.

Hon was twenty-five when the transfer took place and now, at forty-six, was a dual citizen of both Honk Kong and the United States. He had been Wassel's private secretary for twenty-two years and his loyalty was strong.

The instructions he had received from Wassel were, by all measure, strange. The translation of the plans would be no problem, and it did make sense that he would be the logical choice.

Although Chinese was his native tongue, his English had become even better over the years. He did have dual citizenship, so he reasoned that he would just be returning to his childhood home.

Now that he was over the shock of hearing what he had been told, he realized that it was really an honor to have been chosen. The huge salary and bonus helped make up his mind to accept the offer.

After telling Wassel that he agreed, he found that the plans had already been made for him to immediately travel to his new office in Hong Kong.

The Hong Kong legal team had done a superb job setting up the offices and providing staff for the W.H. Shipping Company.

Hon found that the day to day operation was running smoothly. So, he could, on the following Monday, fly to the Hochog Ship Building Company in Monrovia, Liberia.

When he arrived in Monrovia, he was fascinated by the landscape and people. He had never been to the African Continent before, and although he had spent time reading up on it, it was truly a new and different experience for him.

The city was, by all extents modern, and as a coastal town, it would allow him to remain nearby as the ships were being modified.

They had established the initial contact and provided all the necessary financial documentation to the Hochog Ship Building Company, and as a result, Hon was welcomed and treated as a shipping company chief executive should be treated.

When he laid out the plans and specifications there was a moment of concern about the language, but Hon said he would provide the translation to English for them and began to go over the details required.

He explained that all three existing ships were 'small handy size' at about 740 feet long, 80 feet wide and a 28,000 gross tons capacity. As they went over the power requirements and crew quarters, it was a simple task to assure them that the Chinese plan modifications were really not very different than most standard ship construction plans would be.

The only problem was the amount of time it would take for the modifications to be completed. Hon was adamant that they needed be launched in less than 90 days, and the Hochog people wanted at least 120.

It did not sound like it was possible, but Hochog had been doing this for some time and were able to fit out this type of freighter in a very short time.

The only question was about the special direct deck access to a specially built lead lined room 20 feet by twenty feet that was located, on the lowest level of the ship, right above the keel and forward of the main holds. It was to be its only access and would require a material transfer elevator in the access shaft.

Hon would not tell anyone what it is for, only that it was a specific and firm requirement.

23

Monday, 24 September 2018
NSIU Headquarters
Washington, D.C.

Paul, Linda, Jane and Luigi were sitting in the third-floor conference room, each with a cup of coffee in front of them, just looking at each other. It was Luigi who finally said what was on all their minds: "OK, I am about to pull out what hair I have left! We have been trying to find out what the Chinese have hidden on the Suzhou site for over a month and we haven't even got a clue!"

Jane said: "I agree, whatever it is, it is in just such a place that we can't find anyone with access."

Linda spoke up and said: "Let us try a different approach. Maybe it isn't so much what is hidden, but what would they do with it.

"Let us assume that it is a physical item that would need to be transported and, we most likely, would not be happy about it.

"What we do already know is that Harvey Wassel has an ocean shipping fleet and is, somehow, involved with that site. That puts the site location and the shipping method together."

Paul said: "Don't we know that he is planning to increase shipping to and from China and Central America? If so, exactly what is he planning on shipping?"

Linda said: "Paul, that is a good question. I wonder, how he knew about the tokomak site so long before anyone else."

Jane said: "Luigi, awhile ago, you spoke about the Central America countries and their political governments; do you remember?"

Luigi looked up and said: "I do, and maybe that is where we should look. Several of those governments are really questionable about to their ability to rule their own population. Although they are listed as democratic, most have been rather weak in their rise to power. When I was down in Honduras and Costa Rico, a couple of years ago, about the only thing holding them together was tourism from the United States; and that was only so-so."

Paul picked up the topic and said: "You are right Luigi, but Nicaragua and Guatemala are also in a decline as well. I believe those countries are all influenced by agreements with Cuba for the weak protection they supposedly provide.

"However, a big output from those countries is usually drug traffic and illegal aliens through Mexico ultimately up to the US border."

Jane said: "Mexico has worked with our state department and border control recently to reduce a lot of the drug traffic; it is getting better, but it is still a huge problem.

"I understand that Mexico has used some of their interdiction capabilities against the drug trafficking as it comes in, mostly to Guatemala. They maintain a fair amount of control over the international waters even down as far as Panama. We support their efforts, but it is largely under their control."

Linda said: "How are those drugs coming in now? I thought that much of the sea traffic down there was usually tramp freighters from various parts of Asia and India."

Paul said: "OK, so there is a traffic route into Central America that is of a questionable source; so why did Wassel say he was going to move a fair amount of his resources to that route if it is so already controlled?"

Linda said: "Good point Paul, and even adding to that, it all started with the proposed agricultural increase from China. However, agricultural products are already adequate in supply in all of those areas, except Venezuela which is a result of their dictator's incompetence.

"So, I repeat Paul's question, why did Wassel say he was going to move his resources to that route?"

Jane said: "You guys have more experience than I have, but my first impression is that he has made some kind of deal with the Chinese. My question, therefore, would be who in China has he been talking to?"

No one had a comment for that, so they all just stared at one another.

It was Paul who finely broke the silence by saying: "OK, we don't know, so let us think what has happened that would allow us to open an official investigation."

Jane asked: "Who do we want to look at?"

Linda said: "The only one we have a lot of questions about is Harvey Wassel, I think we can start there.

"What I learned from the people in New York is that he has been doing a lot of shipping between the USA and China in both directions; agricultural products mostly to China and multiple products from China to the US.

"All this transportation is negotiated by TWSC executive staff and obviously with the Chinese government's upper staff."

Paul picked up on it and said: "What do we know of him personally?

"We know he has a lot of money, but that isn't a sufficient means for us to look into his business. However, TWSC is a public Company, located in San Francisco, and they are involved in international contracts. They must be transferring funds all over the place to keep those ships sailing. Maybe some of the records are available to the stock holders, so that may be our door into, at least, part of his financial fortune."

Jane said: "I think that the person best suited for this kind of research is Harold, he gets into things I don't even think about."

Linda said she would go and ask if he would begin a trace.

She found him in the coffee room with the admiral. They were discussing information they had received from the CERN scientists and the quality of the protein enhancement that could be expected.

Linda listened for a few moments and realized they were still not sure if it was going to be a viable solution.

When Harold noticed that she was there, both men turned to include her in the discussion. Linda stopped them by saying: "We have been going over everything we know about what was hidden on the Suzhou site and have come to a wall.

"However, we do have a thin thread of an idea, and that is to try and find out why Harvey Wassel has decided to alter his trade routes in favor of the China to Central America routes.

"We want to know if Wassel has had direct communication with the senior Chinese government and wonder if it could be found by looking into TWSC public records and follow the corporate money flow."

Harold and the admiral looked at each other and shrugged. Harold said: "It's a public company, why not?"

"Sounds like a good way to start," said the admiral, "let's give it a try."

Harold stood up and as he was leaving the room said: "I'll get started right away."

24

Friday, 5 October 2018
NSIU Headquarters
Washington, D.C.

Harold Jarrett had been looking at the mountains of documents that are part of the public records for the stock holders of an American corporation. Those records are usually just a printed summery of the detailed corporate decisions regarding the economics of the company, including both income and expenses.

It becomes a little bit more complex when the subject corporation is involved with international trade. Although tax filings of an American corporation are generally kept private and would need a specific legal application for government access, international banking records, can sometimes be more easily viewed. The primary reason for that legal access is to verify that income and expenses between countries are compliant with international trade agreements.

During the past week, Harold had been watching the stock market for unusual changes in general and TWSC's stock value in particular. The market had been slightly gaining, about 0.12% on average; TWSC stock had declined about 0.025% through the same period.

Harold had been speaking to a broker he knew, that was on top of things in the NYC Stock Exchange. He had been able to get copies of the last three months of TWSC stockholders reports. They didn't reveal much, but it did say that three, 28,000 ton freighters had been transferred in ownership to W.H. Shipping Company, in Hong Kong. There was no indication that a purchase or sale, of the ships, was involved and there was no record of any kind of lease arrangement.

That was strange. Harold wondered how and what the reason was for this transfer; and who was the W.H. Shipping Company, in Hong Kong?

He put in a call to Linda and asked her to check with her contacts in NYC and see if they knew anything about them. An hour later, she called him back and said they told her that they had only just heard of them last week. However, they said there were frequently small freighter companies either starting up or shutting down, usually in Asia.

He put in a request to the American Consulate in Hong Kong and asked if they could find out if anything was unusual about this W.H. Shipping Company.

There wasn't much else he could do until he heard back from them, so he decided to accept a long-standing invitation he had to visit some friends in Avalon for the weekend and let his mind rest and relax for a while on the New Jersey shore.

When he got back to his office Monday morning, it was to find that there was a report on his desk from the U.S. Hong Kong Consulate. It stated that the available company information showed that it was a relatively new company filed by a local Hong Kong law firm.

The office address was 8867 Canton Road, in Kowloon, and the Chief Operating Officer was a man named Wayne Hon.

It stated that they had three ships that were crewed by three Chinese Captains and all current crew members were also Chinese. The ships, although only five years old, were being set up for transfer to Liberian Registry. They were currently in Monrovia being modified to accommodate a fifty-container standard freight capacity.

Herold had a strange feeling that something was there that he should know, but he couldn't put a finger on it. He copied the Hong Kong report to Paul, Linda, Jane, and Luigi asking if there was something, that they might know that he had missed.

It was Linda who had thought the name Wayne Hon rang a bell, but she couldn't think where she had heard it before. She decided to ask Emilio Watson if he knew of a shipping company executive named Wayne Hon, Chief Operating Officer of the Hong Kong shipping company.

She placed a call to him, but he wasn't in his office, so she left a message and asked him to call her back.

Fifteen minutes later he called her back and said: "I got your message, and I find it hard to believe that none of us picked up on this before.

"The W.H. in the name of W.H. Shipping Company of Hong Kong stands for Wayne Hon; that is obvious, but what is strange is the only Wayne Hon I ever heard of is the executive secretary to billionaire shipping magnate Harvey Wassel, owner of TWSC."

Linda said: "You have got to be kidding, how would that happen?"

Emilio answered: "I don't know, but I assure you I am going to try and find out. Does this account for an additional competitor in Pacific shipping or just Wassel controlling new routes?"

Linda thanked him and went to look for Harold to tell him about the new twist in the picture. She found him in the conference room with Jane and Paul looking into various ship building companies located in Liberia.

After she told them of the coincidence that the W.H. in the name of W.H. Shipping Company stands for Wayne Hon, the executive secretary to Wassel, they all just looked at each other.

Jane said: "How does that work? Is he still under the employ of TWSC?"

It was Harold who said: "I think that we may have found a link that wasn't there before." Looking over to Jane, he said, "I doubt that he is still under the direct employ of TWSC, but I bet we find that Wassel somehow has a controlling interest in W.H. Shipping Company; albeit probably remote."

Paul asked: "Is there any way we can trace where the funding for this Hong Kong shipping company actually came from?"

Harold sighed and said: "I doubt it, but it may be possible to find something from the international shipping registry. I believe they keep records of all international ship filing documents to assure compliance; that may also include the source of payment for the registration."

It was Paul who came up with an idea that might have slipped through the cracks. He said: "Aren't most international ships insured by a British insurance firm? Maybe they would have a more direct line to who was the beneficiary in case of loss."

Harold looked at Paul and said: "I hadn't thought about the insurance angle, you may be right; I will see if the admiral will approve a request for information from MI-5 (British Intelligence). Since it is a Hong Kong firm, maybe the Brits still keep an eye on what business is happening even though they aren't responsible anymore.

"I know they still have influence with many of the businesses there, and most residents still use British passports. It is an unusual alliance between Hong Kong and mainland China. The 1997 return to China's possession, at the end of the ninety-nine-year British lease, really left a double ruling system; one was communist and the other was capitalist.

As Harold left the room to look for the admiral, the others all decided that they would look into the different ship building companies in Monrovia. Perhaps, they could find what was being done to these ships and why were they being modified.

25

Monday, 8 October 2018
Hochog Ship Building Company
Monrovia, Liberia

Wayne had flown in to Monrovia from Hong Kong last night. He had spent last week going over the day to day operations of the W.H. Shipping Company. All the meetings with the lawyers and getting all the proper maritime documents in order was a huge task.

As he arrived at the Hochog Ship Building Company wharf, he was glad to see that all three ships were on their individual floating dry docks, side by side. He had worried that the Hochog people would not respect him enough to proceed as quickly as he had requested. He should have known, that someone of authority would know that Mr. Wassel was somehow involved.

After an uneventful progress meeting, he went aboard the 'China Girl East', the newest of the three ships, and met with Captain Wo Chang, Captain Hai Ling and Captain Jian Kang. The three captains were very polite and respectful, and completely in control of their own respective commands. They had sent their crews back to China when the project started, and they would all be returning in two weeks for the relaunching of the ships.

The plan was to have the ships ready for sea trials by the first week of November. In the meantime, Wayne would have the registry for each vessel converted to Liberia and get the insurance in place before the relaunch.

The insurance wasn't a problem, because he had declared that the Harvey Wassel Foundation was to be the beneficiary. The British insurance company was the carrier for all of TWSC ships, and when W.H. Shipping Company of Hong Kong applied for coverage, no further questions needed to be asked when they saw the beneficiary's name.

The three captains took their boss on a tour of the 'China Girl East' to show him just how the freight containers would be placed and secured, and the new special access into the forward hull lead lined room and its product mounts. Wayne had seen the plans of course, but he was still impressed with the finished product.

He left the shipyard and as he headed back to his hotel, his cell phone rang. It was Harvey Wassel calling to check on the schedule, he asked: "Are things going as we planned?"

Hon answered: "Yes sir, we have been doing well and are about a full two weeks ahead of schedule.

"I was aboard the 'China Girl East' with all three captains about an hour ago, and they are ready to do sea trials in two and a half weeks."

Wassel asked: "Is the registry completed, and will there be any problem with the insurance?"

Hon said: "All three registrations have been filed and approved. I thought I might have a problem with the insurance, because we are, after all, a small unknown shipping company. However, when they saw that the Wassel Foundation was the beneficiary, they didn't even bat an eye."

Wassel said: "OK, the reason I called is that I got a message from Secretary Lieu that they want to send their first production package to Honduras leaving Shanghai on December 1st.

"He wants to make sure that there will be no problems with the material handling when he sends one of the special packages. He said he will arrange for eighty containers of miscellaneous clothing products to be the reason for the shipment."

Hon answered: "I understand, I will arrange for the crews to returned to Monrovia next week, and then we can push for the required sea trials as soon as the ships are relaunched.

"We can sail on November 6th. It will take about fourteen days to get back to Hong Kong and one more day to Shanghai. If we allow for one day of loading in Shanghai, we should be OK. Once they leave

Shanghai, it will take fourteen days to Puerto Cortés, Honduras. That will give us an eight-day cushion just in case there are any problems."

Wassel said: "Very well, I'll tell Lieu that is the plan."

26

Wednesday, 17 October 2018
NSIU Headquarters
Washington, D.C.

Harold was sitting at his desk when his phone rang. It was Nigel Donaldson calling him from MI-5 in London. Harold and Nigel had been friends for several years; ever since they worked together on a Russian spy case that involved both the USA and the UK.

"Harold you dog, I haven't heard anything from you in over a year; how have you been, are you still doing secret stuff?" asked Nigel.

Harold, with a great big smile on his face, said: "I try not to let British intelligence know what is going on, it would be all over the news within minutes."

"I thought it was the United States Congress that couldn't keep anything secret."

Harold asked: "Have you ever listened to the 'Prime Minister's Questions' on TV, you might wonder if anyone in England can even pour tea without letting the opposition insult them."

Nigel laughed and said: "Opposition my foot, at least we can talk to each other; not like the American political parties that just can't get anything done!"

Harold said: "You still can't get over the fact that we kicked your butt out of our country back in 1776."

Nigel laughing said: "OK, enough. I have a message here saying that you need our expert advice once again; what is happening?"

Harold, with a more serious tone, said: "Do you remember the China nuclear project that was talked about at the UN a few months ago?"

Nigel said: "Do you mean that Tokomak food process experiment that came from an idea that was first explained by CERN? I remember it."

Harold said: "Well, we have been following it as closely as we can, and we think China is using it as a blind to hide some sort of other project.

"Actually, we do know that they have a large hidden area on the site, we just don't know what their plan for it is."

Nigel said: "The only information we have is what was explained by the UN and that doesn't tell us much. What is it, that you think, we can tell you that you don't already know?"

Harold took a deep breath and said: "Well, we have found another angle, and it involves ocean shipping.

"When the food process was explained, it came to light that our Midwest farmers might be negatively impacted by the potential change in production. That, in itself is a concern, but without any proof of the concept, there is no real reason to change existing production and transportation methods.

"However, one major ocean shipping company has done just that, and they have already made several big changes."

Nigel said: "We noticed that Harvey Wassel had issued a statement that he was reducing his pacific fleet. Is he the one?"

Harold answered: "Yes. However, that reduction is coupled with several other actions he seems to have taken. For example; he recently has had a lot of communication with Beijing in regard to their shipping needs, and he seems to be accommodating them.

"Meanwhile, a new small ocean shipping company has appeared. It is the W.H. Shipping Company of Hong Kong. Have you heard of it?"

Nigel said: "We still have a fair amount of influence in Hong Kong, as I'm sure you know, and we keep an eye on anything that may involve international relations.

"So, yes I have heard about it. The W.H. stands for a man named Wayne Hon, who is listed on the filing documents as the Chief Operating Officer. They are new and only have three small 'Handy' size container type freighters.

"They are Liberian registered and have projected contract routes between Hong Kong and Shanghai, to Puerto Cortés, Honduras in Central America."

"OK" said Harold, "did you know that Wayne Hon is, or was, the executive secretary for Harvey Wassel?"

Nigel slowly said: "Really?"

"Yes", said Harold, "really; that does make it a bit interesting, doesn't it?"

"So, does Wassel own the W.H. Shipping Company?" asked Nigel.

Harold answered: "That is one of the questions I wanted to ask you. A new Hong Kong based company with all documents and filings taken care of by a well-known Hong Kong legal firm seems to lean that way.

"I thought that you might find out something for us, and that is, who is the insurance carrier? Also, who is the beneficiary?"

Nigel said: "Good point, most likely the carrier is here in London, most maritime policies are. I'll check and get back to you as soon as I find out."

As Harold hung up, he began to think that he was missing something. Why would a new small ocean shipping company take three small "Handy" type freighters all the way to Liberia from Hong Kong to have them serviced and to change registration?

There were a number of ship servicing companies right there in the Hong Kong area that could do whatever job was needed, and national registration was easily done with Lawyers and even online.

Having ships registered in Liberia was understandable, as almost half of the world's merchant ships were registered there. It allowed for open registries and, along with Panama and Marshall Islands flags, it accounted for almost 40% of the entire world's freight shipping fleet.

But the cost of moving three ships halfway around the world and back was huge, so why did they do it?

He thought that they must have had some modification done to the ships that they didn't want known about, and that it would have been linked to China if it had been done in that area. What could that have been?

There were quite a few ship building companies along the coast of Africa, particularly in Liberia. Harold would try to find which one was actually doing the work.

He began his search looking for a company that was capable of handling all three ships at the same time, was reliable, and was near an international airport. That narrowed the search a little and the only one, large enough, was the Hochog Ship Building Company in Monrovia.

He wanted to know what was being done to these three ships, but without access to the ship building company, was not sure how he could find out.

He did, however, know Captain Stephen Lion; the previous commander of the destroyer whom he had sailed under when he first joined the navy four years previously. The Captain, a pleasant man who had always been a friend to Harold, was currently assigned shore duty at Norfolk, Virginia Naval Station. He was overall director of special work projects for many ships that needed to be placed in floating dry docks for bottom inspection and service.

Harold placed a call to the Captain's office and made an appointment for Friday morning. He knew it was a long shot, but he wanted to ask the Captain for his opinion on the best way to find out, if possible, what was being done at a civilian ship building company in another country.

It was a three-and-a-half-hour drive from Washington to Norfolk, so Harold was on the road early, well before the morning traffic was starting. It was a pleasant drive, and as the sun came up over the Virginia countryside, he was looking forward to seeing the Captain and hoped his schedule would let him enjoy a little time with him.

Captain Lion was sitting at his desk when Harold was ushered in and smiled and said: "Well Lieutenant, it has been a while."

Harold at attention, saluted and said: "Good morning Captain, so very nice to see you and thank you for letting me come."

The Captain said: "It is good to see you Harold. Please sit down and tell me what Navy Security wants from a sea going Captain who is stuck on shore!"

Harold smiled and said: "I believe, sir, they keep you here because you are so very good at what you do to help keep the Navy afloat."

The Captain smiled and said: "I am told that if I can put up with the land-based operation for six more months, I will get a new sea going command and, maybe, a star; I'll believe it if and when it happens. In the meantime, all I can do is take ships out of the water and paint their damn bottoms!"

Harold laughed and said: "I do have a question sir, that you may be able to help me with concerning ship building and maintenance; although not military, and not in our navy.

"We have been following some commercial shipping activities that involve international freight transportation between China and us. It involves a potential result from nuclear activities the Chinese are working on."

Captain Lion said: "I presume you are referring to the Tokomak fusion food enhancement project they are putting together."

Harold answered: "Yes sir, that is where it all started, but we have found that it may be more than what has been reported.

"It seems that there may be a hidden part of the project that involves commercial shipping to and from China and Central America. We don't know what it involves, but it is strange that there is a new small shipping company from Hong Kong that appears to be the designated carrier for that route.

"It also is a bit strange that one of the world's largest ocean freight carriers has a possible connection with that new company. However, it is the unusual work that is being done at the Hochog Ship Building Company in Monrovia that has our interest.

"Our question is, what would be the reason to sail three small empty freighters, half way around the world, to have some special work done that could not have been done in a local Hong Kong shipyard?"

Captain Lion said: "I assume you are asking me to get you an answer for that question?"

"Yes sir, that is what I hope you can help us find an answer to."

The Captain leaned back in his chair and said: "Well, I believe you might have come to the right place.

"Two years ago, a brushing incident between a Japanese auto carrier and one of our amphibious transport dock ships occurred in some rough weather off the Liberian coast. The Japanese ship was literally blown off course by the high winds and drifted into our ships path.

"There was very little contact and there was no damage to the Japanese freighter, but we took a bit of a hit to the starboard rear quarter breaking a few rails and tearing up about ten feet of deck."

Harold said: "How come that never hit the news, one would think the news hawks would be all over it?"

Captain Lion said: "There was no real damage and the storm was really the culprit; also, we didn't want to have the Japanese captain disciplined for what was a questionable incident. Our captain was exonerated from any responsibility, and we just let it go as weather related.

"Since we were right off the coast of Monrovia, it made sense to have both vessels checked and repaired by the local ship yard, and that was the Hochog Ship Building Company."

Harold said: "Were you able to talk to the repair people at the company?"

The Captain said: "Yes, that is why I said you might have come to the right place. I flew over to Monrovia to inspect the damage and the repair effort.

"It really was almost nothing, but we did the necessary documentation for both the Japanese and our records, and everything went fine. The Hochog people were very pleasant, assigned no blame, and repaired our damage in less than two days.

I enjoyed working with the Hochog chief engineer, Wolfram Akola. He is the largest black man I have ever known, and probably the best structural engineer I've ever met. I wish he worked for us."

Harold asked: "Would it be possible to find out what was being done to the three 'Handy' freighters from Hong Kong, without breaking any rules?"

The Captain smiled and said: "Of course not, that would be a terrible breach of ethics!" Then with a sly smile, said: "I think it is time for me to call my friend Wolfram and see how he is doing and ask him again if he would like to come to America and head up some of the work here. I know he will refuse, his wife has him completely under her control and she likes it there."

After thanking and leaving the Captain, Harold, on his way back to Washington, thought to himself that it was funny how things that don't seem to have any connection with one another often lead to a result never anticipated.

27

Tuesday, 30 October 2018
Tokomak Nuclear Site
Near Suzhou, China

The time had come to begin the testing of the Helix in the Tokomak and load the plasma for the first time.

Dr. Lee and his staff were all briefed and in position to start the electromagnetic field that would contain the free particles once the fusion had occurred.

The start-up would begin after the cooling towers were activated and set to contain the heat from the atomic fusion process once it had started.

The tests were to assure that all the components of the process would stand up to intense forces that would occur within the various components.

Dr. Lee, with approval from the General Secretary, had invited two European researchers to come from CERN and witness the startup and initial tests.

The tests went well, and each component performed as intended.

A check and careful monitoring of the dozen or so dosimeters showed no unusual radiation, so all was good.

The testing that would continue for the next few weeks would show a ninety-three percent efficiency factor. It was a little lower than they wanted, but good enough for them to continue with the next stage of the process, the food enhancement.

At the same time these tests were going on, the Beijing Scientific Institute began starting the Hadron Collider.

All the testing and initial startup procedures were going well, and it was time to try and stabilize the remaining plasma and expose the 'Quarks' to certain animal and vegetable molecules, to see if it would substantially increase the production of proteins in those items.

That was, after all, the reason for this whole project.

Dr. Lee was very nervous, his reputation and all he stood for was now in the laboratory where biologists were looking at the result of the process. It came out that it was successful and the increase in food source protein was almost thirty percent.

It was better than he had hoped for. It had been almost two years, and now his reputation would stand up to the world's view.

The day to day operation of the facility would be handed over to the staff he had assembled, and they would take care of the logistics necessary to work out the food production increase.

The representatives from CERN invited him to become a member of their research team and asked if he would come to Switzerland and present the results to them.

It would be a chance for Dr. Lee to continue with his effort to improve the world's food production, but he wasn't sure he would be allowed to leave China.

He had been under constant surveillance from Secretary Lieu's security force for more than three months, and knew that everything he had said or done, in that time, was logged recorded and reviewed by Lieu's people.

Lieu was not a fool; he knew that Dr. Lee was a potential security threat and that, if he was allowed to leave his control, China's hidden nuclear project could likely be exposed.

The surveillance had been tight, with Lieu's people intercepting and monitoring all forms of communication the good Doctor had. He realized right away his access to the outside world had been effectively cut off, and that even communication with Lijuan was a danger if she asked him the wrong question.

He realized that his call to Carl from the train, back in July, had been a lucky break. Carl was a very bright man and had, obviously, understood that there was a situation developing that could be dangerous.

From the letters and e-mails he received from Lijuan, it was obvious that Carl had been able to inform Lijuan that there was a danger and she could not ask him any specific questions. So, she had kept him informed about the archeological research project she was involved with and that she was also going to teach several courses at CTU along with Carl.

He figured that he could risk a call on the phone and speak to both Carl and Lijuan and tell them of the success of the Tokomak project and of his invitation to visit CERN. It was, after all, the height of his career, and only natural that he would want his daughter to know of it.

The call went better than he had hoped. It was Carl who answered the phone, and Dr. Lee told him of the successful events including the invitation to go to Switzerland.

Carl said: "That is wonderful Sir, the timing may be very good. But, let me put Lijuan on, she wants to tell you something."

Lijuan, almost bouncing up and down, took the phone and said excitedly: "Papa, Carl told me that he spoke to you when we first came to America; and he has asked me to marry him; and I said yes!"

Dr. Lee said, with a loving tone in his voice: "My darling daughter, I did speak to Carl back then and I approve completely. Have you set a date yet?"

She answered: "No, not yet, but we want to have the wedding here in Texas at the University if we can.

"I know that you and I are the only ones left in our family and Carl has only his mother and father. So, we have been thinking that the people that I was rescued with in Syria, and the members of the team that rescued us, along with Carl's parents and you would be a perfect size group for the wedding."

Dr. Lee laughing, said: "That may work well, particularly if it can be done at the same time I would need to go to Switzerland."

Dr. Lee asked to speak to Carl again and as Lijuan handed him the phone she could hardly contain her enthusiasm.

Carl said: "Thank you for your approval Sir, I will try to keep her happy and safe."

Dr. Lee answered: "I know you will, congratulations. Please let me know the date as soon as you can, it may be a bit difficult to coordinate it with my on-going responsibilities, but I would not want to miss my only daughter's wedding."

Carl said: "I understand Sir, with all that is happening in our lives now, please know that our short e-mails and notes are only to get things organized and we are so very grateful for your support."

After they hung up the call, Carl turned to Lijuan, took her in his arms and hugged her tight. He said: "Sweetheart, I must tell you that there was more to that phone call than just the joy of telling your father that we are going to wed.

"I want you to see something that tells us someone was listening in on our call."

He held the satellite phone out to her and pointed to the little flashing "IC" in the corner of the screen and said: "Those flashing letters tell us that the call was being monitored and recorded as we spoke; and that it was done from his end.

"I am telling you this, because it is obvious that he could still be in danger, and that we cannot put him at risk with any questions other than those of our wedding plans.

"So, let's select the date you wish, and we will begin to set up all the plans."

Lijuan looked into Carl's eyes, and said: "I love you, and thank you for all the care you give me. I understand that you are also concerned about my father, and I too am concerned.

"We will be very careful with what we do and say, but it is our wedding; and it will be our life together. I believe we should schedule the wedding for Saturday, December 15th, will that allow us to get everything done?"

Carl kissed her and said: "We will make it work!"

Back in Suzhou, Dr. Lee sat quietly and thought about the phone call to Lijuan and Carl.

He had a feeling of joy and contentment about his daughter and her future. It couldn't have been better; she was with the man she loved, he would protect her, keep her in America, and he knew they were both aware of the situation that he was in.

They may not have known exactly what was happening, but Carl had the keen insight to realize that there was something about the nuclear facility that was not what it should be, and that someone in the Chinese government was watching his every move.

He realized that the opportunity created by his daughter's upcoming wedding, coupled with the successful food project and the request for him to present the results to CERN was strong, if he could play it well.

The best way to do that was to go directly to the General Secretary and lay out the positive impact the world will give to China when he presented the results. He knew that there were negotiations on-going between Beijing and Washington, and China's negotiating position was now, perhaps, enhanced.

His laptop computer 'chirped' telling him an e-mail had just arrived. He got up walked over to it and read the short simple note: 'We have set the date and it is December 15th, love Lijuan.'

28

Friday, 9 November 2018
General Secretary's Office
Beijing, China

Dr. Lee had called Beijing and asked for a meeting with the General Secretary. He wanted to tell him about the excellent results obtained from the tests at the Tokomak food enhancement project. He knew that all his conversations had been monitored by Secretary Lieu, and that there would always be tension between them. But he now, for the moment anyway, had the upper hand. But he needed to be very careful that he didn't over play it.

As with the previous meeting, Secretary Lieu was present at the meeting with the General Secretary; but it was Dr. Lee who had the control this time.

He spoke about the successful test results and the indication that the future food enhancement production looked as if it was going to be as good as predicted. He said that the inclusion of the representatives from CERN, at the initial tests, had been inspirational. They of course knew the actual process, but the General Secretary's invitation, to actually witness it in operation, was brilliant.

He told the Secretary that the CERN observers had asked if he would come to Switzerland and join with them in the continuing research.

Before Lieu could say anything, he also said that he thought a formal presentation to the United Nations Security Council was very appropriate. Since they had been following it so closely, it would be a victory in China's effort to relax tensions.

Lieu spoke up at that point and told the Secretary that maybe it was too soon for all that to happen. After all, the necessary production and transportation of the food products was barely begun, and Dr. Lee would need to be here to oversee the operation.

Dr. Lee said: "Actually, everything is already in place, and I also have another reason to go to America and Switzerland.

"My daughter told me the other day, that she has become engaged to a young man who is also a history teacher at a University in Texas. The wedding is scheduled for December 15th, at the University, and I really would like to walk my daughter down the aisle."

He had known that the General Secretary was a family man, with two grown children and several grandchildren. By playing on the General Secretary's emotions, he succeeded in his proposal in spite of Lieu's protests.

Lieu wasn't happy about having Dr. Lee out of his area of control and made a big mistake by voicing it without thinking where he was. Lieu said: "I don't think you can do this trip. We have a number of things going on that need be done and we can't protect you while those items are on-going."

The General Secretary looked up at Lieu and said: "Exactly what are you protecting Dr. Lee from?"

Lieu was in trouble; he hadn't informed the Secretary of the surveillance he had placed on Dr. Lee, and now he had indicated that there was something that threatened him.

His thoughts went back to that first meeting when Dr. Lee first exposed the radio activity levels to the General Secretary and Lieu had played them down. He had thought the hidden project was going to be exposed, and it was his project.

Lieu answered the Secretary's question: "Dr. Lee is known internationally as a Chinese nuclear physicist; he could be at risk of capture or assassination if he travels out of our area of protection."

Both Dr. Lee and the General Secretary sat and just stared at Lieu. Their thoughts were similar, both wondered what had happened to Lieu that he would make such a stupid statement.

It was the Secretary who had the greater concern, however. He had allowed Lieu and his department access to the Suzhou nuclear site for his hidden storage and weapons factory, and now here he was acting as if he had control of the whole project.

It was Lieu who had been working on the ocean shipping contracts, and he hadn't informed the General Secretary of his intention to move low level 'dirty bombs' to Central American countries. It was with Minister Fu Li Meilin and General Dong Chao Jing that those plans had been developed.

Well, perhaps General Jing wasn't completely on board. He hadn't openly protested the plan, but he hadn't really endorsed it either.

There was always a feeling that General Jing really wanted Lieu's position. He would use all the political power he could muster to withhold his support of the plan, if he knew that the General Secretary wasn't aware of it.

Lieu had told them that a plan set forward from the general council was what was behind the project, but it really had been his own idea.

Now he was going to have Dr. Lee loose in the world without any control over what he told everybody. His only hope was based on the fact that Lee didn't know what was being done in those hidden rooms. He would have to rely on that thread.

In an effort to recover from his mistake, Lieu said: "I am only concerned with his safety, but of course, he must be the one to travel and spread the good news to the world. It just is we need his expert opinion as well, but he must be the one to go."

As the meeting broke up, with Lieu walking out first, the General Secretary and Dr. Lee looked at each other and shrugged.

The Secretary told him that it may be possible for them to travel to the United States together, as he will be meeting with the American President in the White House in a few weeks; maybe, if the timing works, as Dr. Lee addressed the United Nations.

29

Friday, 16 November 2018
W. H. Ocean Shipping Company
Offices, Hong Kong

The three empty 'Handy' Container ships; 'China Girl East', 'Lazy Red Dragon', and 'Iris in the Mist', had left Monrovia five days previously and were now headed back to Hong Kong. Before they put to sea, they had each taken on fifty thousand gallons of sea water as ballast to assure they could safely handle any rough seas that they might encounter.

They calculated they would arrive in Hong Kong on the 25th of November on the morning tide. They were currently approaching the Suez Canal and were scheduled through it in one long day.

A call from Wayne Hon was answered by Captain Wo Chang, aboard the 'China Girl East'. He was pleased to tell is employer that all three ships were a little ahead of schedule and were sailing smoothly with no problems.

He told Wayne that Captain Hai Ling, aboard the 'Lazy red Dragon', and Captain Jian Kang, aboard 'Iris in the Mist', were both in line directly behind him.

With their Liberian registry, and flying the Liberian flag, they were cleared through Suez Canal Port control with no questions.

Wayne told the Captain that he would arrange three anchorages' in Hong Kong Harbor, and they could pump out the sea water from the ballast tanks when they arrived.

It would be Captain Wo Chang, and the 'China Girl East' that would proceed to Shanghai on Monday the 26th of November.

The 'Lazy Red Dragon', and 'Iris in the Mist', were being scheduled to transport 48 Containers each from Hong Kong to Haiphong, Vietnam the following Wednesday.

After speaking with his Captain, Wayne put through a call to Harvey Wassel and told him that the plan was proceeding, and he would be ready for the instructions from Shanghai.

Wassel explained that Wayne would be receiving instructions directly from a General Dong Chao Jing with directions as to where Captain Wo Chang, and the 'China Girl East' would tie up and receive her cargo. Sailing schedule was set to leave Shanghai on December 1st and sail to Puerto Cortés, Honduras in Central America with arrival on the 14th of December.

Back in Washington, Harold received a phone call from Captain Stephen Lion. It seems that his engineering friend, Wolfram Akola at the Hochog Shipyard in Monrovia, was considering a change of employment and a new life in the United States.

Harold said: "I thought you told me he was the best ship engineer you ever knew; did something happen in Monrovia that makes him want to leave the Hochog Shipyard? I believe you said he was at his wife's command about living in Liberia."

The Captain, laughing said: "He was in a great humor, his wife is pregnant and had told him that she didn't want her child to be born in Africa, and she wanted him to consider a move to the United States.

"I told him he would probably be permitted to emigrate to America; he had wanted to do that for years, but she had always wanted to stay in Liberia where they had always been.

"I didn't tell him I would sponsor them in their effort to become citizens, but of course, I will. I have some influence over at Newport News Shipbuilding, and it would mean we would have a superior ship engineer available whenever we needed one."

Harold said: "Will that change your plans of going back to sea in the next few months?"

Captain Lion said: "No, but I would feel a lot better with the knowledge that the Navy would have access to an engineer who really knows what he is doing and would work so well with the people around him.

"That is only part of the reason I was calling you however; you asked me if I could find out why a civilian company would move three small freighters halfway around the world to have some work done that could have been done locally.

"Well, I put some of my integrity in a drawer, and asked Wolfram what was so special about those three ships. He told me that it was an unusual request that had been made, for they really only wanted each ship to have a special isolated four hundred square foot hold installed just above the keel.

"What made it unusual, was that there was only one deck level entrance freight elevator access to the hold. Also, the entire hold and shaft were lined with a quarter inch of lead sheathing."

Harold said: "Why would they do that; it must mean that they are planning to transport something that could contaminate the surrounding area?"

The Captain continued: "Even more than that, the plans for the installation were written in Chinese, and it was the W.H. Shipping Company CEO, Wayne Hon himself, who provided the on-site translation."

Harold, sitting back in his chair, was astounded: "You mean that Hon was, himself, in Monrovia while the modification was being done?"

Captain Lion said: "Apparently!"

Harold asked: "Did your engineer say anything else about the project?"

"Only that each hold had four special holding clamps attached to the deck; I suppose to lock whatever was being loaded into a fixed position and prevent it from shifting around if they were caught in ruff seas.

"I agree that the project was a strange one; and remember, the total dimension is smaller than that of a standard shipping container": Answered Captain Lion.

Harold, with more questions in his head than answers, said: "I admit I am at a loss as to what or why this was being done. The only thing I can think of is that whatever they plan to load must be very dangerous if it got loose. Do you have any other thoughts about it?"

Captain Lion answered: "Funny you should ask; I have seen this type of concern only on vessels that carry nuclear radioactive materials that are being transported and need be very carefully handled. However, that has always been on Navy ships from some major nuclear capacity country; never before on any other type of commercial vessel I ever heard of."

Harold thanked the Captain for the information and told him he would let him know what he found out if and when it all came together.

After the call, Harold just sat and let his mind go over the many items he had found. There were a lot from many sources, and he needed time to put them together.

He knew it was time for him to start an outline and assemble the various known factual items and observations into a source that everyone at NSIU could look at and discuss.

He thought that he would need a little time to relax for a few days before he began however; so, he called his friends at the Jersey shore in Avalon and asked if he could come for a short visit, just to clear his mind.

30

Monday, 19 November 2018
NSIU Headquarters
Washington, D.C.

Harold walked into NSIU on Monday morning, well relaxed after three days of rest and an easy visit with his friends at the shore.

He walked over to the coffee bar and found there was a box of donuts open next to the coffee machine. He got his coffee and snared two donuts on his way to his office. He didn't have a desk in his office, just a fair-sized table with a very comfortable swivel chair, a laptop computer and a phone.

He had three guest chairs, for conversations when he needed to have them, but mostly it was his thinking room, and he usually was alone as he worked.

He began to enter the known items into his computer as he arranged the known order of discovery:

- 1 – Early in April, on the 10th, the NSA had heard rumors of the Chinese building a nuclear site in Suzhou, China.
- 2 – NASA recovers photos of Suzhou construction site from a doomed satellite, sends them to NSA and to UNAG at the United Nations.
- 3 – Harold and Jane go to visit Dr. Cootes from the DOE, learn about Dr. Lin Chang Lee from China, and the CERN symposium in Hong Kong. Dr. Lee was the likely head of the Chinese nuclear food production project.

- 4 - UNAG gets confirmation of the Suzhou nuclear, Tokomak, food production project site from Chinese UN ambassador.
- 5 – A very unusual special request is made by the DOD for the NSIU seal team to take down a terror cell in Aleppo, Syria; and capture the cell leader. After the successful operation, a second terror cell takedown in Lattakia, Syria was requested and also succeeded; with the recovery of a group of archeologists that had been previously captured in Turkey.
- 6 – A coincidence that one of the archeologists was the daughter of Dr. Lin Chang Lee, head of the Suzhou nuclear project. Her successful rescue, along with all the others, was appreciated by each of the involved countries.
- 7 – A romantic relationship develops between Dr. Lee's daughter, Lijuan, with one of the seal team members, Petty Officer Carl Muskin, who offers to end his Navy career to avoid any impropriety. He returns to his previous career as a history professor at CTU.
- 8 – Dr. Lee, along with the Chinese delegation addresses the UN Security Council about the Tokomak food enhancement project that he is the director of in Suzhou.
- 9 – NSIU investigator, Linda DeSanto, learns about an international investment opportunity that may lead to potential changes in USA China shipping of food products.
- 10 – Dr. Lee and his daughter travel, on a vacation trip, to Washington DC to let Dr. Lee meet Carl Muskin. Also, he meets the NSIU admiral, along with Jane and Harold in a social meeting with Dr. Lee where he expresses his appreciation for the rescue in Syria.
- 11 – Lijuan, who had returned to China to get a work visa to the USA, comes back to the USA and goes to Texas to try and get an archeological project started in Arizona.
- 12 - Carl receives a short, strange, phone call from Dr. Lee; where he asks Carl to keep Lijuan safely in America. Carl, realizing there might be a situation that he doesn't know about, immediately calls NSIU and speaks to the admiral and tells him all about the phone call.

- 13 – Linda goes back to NYC and meets with the four people who were the first to know about the food production project in China. She learns that a major ocean shipping company, TWSC, was strangely announcing and making changes to their USA China shipping routes. New routes would include shipping from China to several Central American countries

- 14 – Paul, after thinking something must be happening at the Suzhou site that was being hidden, asks Jane to go with him to NASA Johnson Space Center and take a careful look at aerial satellite photos of the site. They find that a large area in the center of the site had been hidden under camouflage netting and was finally revealed as a finished park setting. They could not identify what had been built and hidden beneath the ground.

- 15 – News that the unusual reduction in shipping, that is revealed by billionaire Harvey Wassel, is found to be connected with the formation of the W.H. Shipping Company of Hong Kong. The W.H. stood for Wayne Hon, Wassel's executive secretary.

- 16 – Wayne Hon travels to Liberia to have his three ships, 'China Girl East', 'Lazy Red Dragon', and 'Iris in the Mist', modified and registered there. The modifications were unusual and were obviously being hidden since they could have been done locally.

- 17 – It was found that the modification to each of the three small freighters was for the installation of a lead lined small hold. The design for these special holds was obviously done in China, because the drawing details were written in Chinese. Wayne Hon himself did the translation for the shipyard; and they were most likely built for the transport of explosive radioactive materials.

As Harold sat and read through the outline a second time, it was becoming obvious to him that there was some kind of unusual action being done by the Chinese. It also looked like it could involve a potential low-level nuclear capacity being provided to several unstable Central American governments.

With that thought, he figured that now it was time for the admiral to see the outline.

31

Thursday, 28 November 2018
General Secretary's Office
Beijing, China

The General Secretary, along with several other ministers, including Defense Secretary Lieu, Assistant Defense Secretary Chen Hui Sing, and cabinet officials, Liu Gen Feng, Fu Li Meilin, and General Dong Chao Jing, discussed the upcoming trip that was scheduled for the week beginning December 12th in the United States.

Dr. Lee was scheduled to address the UN General Assembly on Thursday the 13th, about the positive results from the 'Tokomak Food Production Project'. The General Secretary was also scheduled to address them following Dr. Lee's presentation, with the indication that China was moving in the direction of improving Asian and Indian food supplies, long needed to improve the poverty levels in that part of the world.

The schedule then had the General Secretary meeting with the President of the United States at the Whitehouse for two days beginning on Monday the 17th. That meeting would follow discussions between the undersecretaries of both countries regarding future trade agreements.

After his address to the UN General Assembly, Dr. Lee was free to travel to Texas for his daughter's wedding, and then on to Switzerland to visit with the scientists at CERN.

It was this last part of the itinerary that was a concern of Secretary Lieu.

The big worry for Lieu was that somehow the General Secretary would learn of the 'Dirty Bombs' before he completed his meetings in the United States. However, once the weapons were in the hands of the Central American countries, there was a definite area of plausible deniability. It was even a strong possibility that the guilt would be placed at the doors of Cuba and Russia.

It wouldn't matter of course; the goal was to force the United States to spend resources on stabilizing those weak Central American countries, while China gained a strong position by controlling Pacific Ocean shipping.

But with Dr. Lee out of his immediate control, there was a fear that the knowledge he had of the secret hidden weapon assembly and storage facility, on the grounds of the Suzhou site, would become known. That could lead to a failure of Lieu's private agenda.

Lieu had planned that the Chinese Communist Party would blame the General Secretary for the destruction of East/West relations and the increase of nuclear proliferation in the world. They would want him removed and immediately replaced.

Lieu believed that he was actually the one in place to take over the General Secretary's position; and then he could guide China to be even more powerful. He was so blinded by his own ambition; he couldn't see that it would probably be himself who would actually be the one blamed.

The loading of 'China Girl East' with four fully assembled 'Dirty Bombs' was taking place as they were meeting in Beijing; it was scheduled to sail on Saturday, December 1st. Both Fu Li Meilin, and General Dong Chao Jing had wanted to delay the shipment until after the General Secretary's trip was completed, but the government representatives from both Honduras and El Salvador wouldn't have it. In the end, it was Secretary Lieu who agreed to let the ship sail as scheduled.

Most of their discussion, however, was in an effort to foresee the reaction that could take place as the anticipated changes in food production became known.

The Chinese would now, as a result of the nuclear food enhancement capability, be in a stronger position to get a reduction of the tariffs that the United States had placed on imports from China. The power of this action would also become more obvious as a reduction in the Midwest farm exports from America to Asia began to happen.

The Communist Party of China officials were being careful to not overplay this projected change. To push too hard, would not be wise; after all, the United States was still the most powerful country on earth, and it had many ways to counter another's over powerful ambitions.

It was the General Secretary's position, that it would be best to try and keep as much of the agricultural imports from the United States as possible; while, at the same time create extended export of the nuclear enhanced foods to the remote poverty areas of Asia, India, and Africa. That way, it would be a slow change and eventually become a powerful negotiating tool for the Chinese to export even more general products.

As the discussion continued, Lieu remained unusually quiet. His position was quite different than the General Secretary's, he wanted to force the United States into a position that they would be seen as overpowering small insignificant governments by the rest of the world. He believed China would then become recognized as the world's new major ruling power.

General Dong Chao Jing sat quietly and listened to the conversation. He was becoming more and more concerned that he had picked the wrong side. He noted the silence from Lieu and listened to the positive input projection from the General Secretary.

It was a concern growing in his mind that if Lieu's plan was successful, and China's part in it was exposed to the world, it could easily lead to war.

General Jing had always been a thoughtful military leader and had, as a result, the support of the many troops he commanded over the years. He was for China, of that there was no doubt, but it was the people he was in charge of that was his primary concern.

He had always believed in creating situations that would help strengthen his country's influence throughout the world; but, just maybe, he had backed the wrong horse in this race.

As he looked over at Defense Secretary Lieu, the thought came to his mind that allowing Lieu's action to go as planned, was just wrong. He was, however, boxed in; he couldn't go against Lieu, and he couldn't tell the General Secretary.

He knew about Lieu's surveillance of Dr. Lee, and he was sure that Dr. Lee also knew of it. Maybe there was a way.

What if he could let Dr. Lee find out what was planned, without him knowing it was he that 'leaked' the actual information about the plan?

Dr. Lee was already aware that it was radioactive materials being kept in the hidden area. It was that discovery and disclosure to the General Secretary that first made Lieu follow Lee's every move.

Dr. Lee had several times telephoned his daughter in Texas, but he also knew that those conversations were being monitored. However, Dr. Lee's daughter was engaged to a United States ex-navy seal who still had access to his former commander.

Was there a way the pertinent information regarding the 'Dirty Bombs' schedule and purpose could get to Lijuan's fiancé?

There was really only one chance, but the risk was very high, and timing was not in their favor. He would carefully prepare a note that he could have passed to Dr. Lee, without him knowing from whom or where it came from. It would then be up to Dr. Lee to get the information to someone, with a source that would know what to do.

It was his best chance to fix the problem, before it got out of hand.

32

Monday, 3 December 2018
NSIU Headquarters
Washington, D.C.

As General Jing left Beijing, on his way back to Suzhou, he thought how he could pass the word to Dr. Lee. A simple innocuous note that told the story was all it would be.

He stopped at his office, took out a piece of parchment and wrote: '*The ocean waitress China Girl East is bringing a Suzhou dinner for the Honduras President, it should be there on December 14th, to Feed the Hungry Atom*'.

Sometimes the best way to deliver something, was the easiest, he wrote Dr. Lee's name and office address on the envelope and gave it to a young soldier in his office and told him to give to Dr. Lee's secretary.

Dr. Lee was at his desk when his secretary brought his mail, including the note, and he began to sort through it. As he read the note, an understanding of what was going on became very clear to him.

His choice would be, did he risk sending this to Carl, with the hope he would pass it on, or was it a trap that he should ignore. The answer was simple, he couldn't ignore it.

He took the easiest way to do it, enclosed the note in an engagement card and addressed it to Lijuan in Texas. After making sure it had the proper postage, he simply walked past a post office on his way home and dropped it in the box.

Monday morning, Carl picked up the mail at the college post office and saw there was a card from China addressed to Lijuan. He smiled, as he thought his future father in law was trying to make life for Lijuan as normal as possible. He walked over to Lijuan's apartment and handed her the card, saying: "I think your father is beginning to realize that you are really going to get married."

As he was leaving, Lijuan called out: "Carl! Wait, what is this note about?"

Turning back to her, Carl took and read the note. His investigative training kicked in and he realized immediately what this was.

He said: "Lijuan, come take a walk with me, it is a lovely day in the park."

As they walked to a remote section of the park, Carl said to Lijuan: "Your father just took an incredible risk. By sending this to you, he is letting us know that something has happened and wants to assure it becomes known while something can still be done about it."

Lijuan said: "Carl, he knows all about you and your connection with the navy, and he knew I would show this to you. Do you think he wants you to get this information to Washington?"

Carl said: "Sweetheart, I am sure that is exactly what he wants us to do. I believe he took the simplest and probably the safest method of letting us know; being fully aware that everything he does is monitored, he simply mailed it in an engagement card and dropped it off at a post office."

Lijuan asked: "Shouldn't you call your people in Washington and let them know of it?"

Carl leaned down and kissed her, saying: "That is one of the reasons I love you Lijuan, you know just what I must do, and tell me it is the right thing to do."

As they sat on the park bench, Carl pulled out his satellite phone, put through a coded call to the NSIU, and spoke to Lieutenant Jarrett.

Harold sat at his desk and thought about the call he had from Carl. He agreed with Carl that Lijuan's father had taken a huge risk sending that note to his daughter. The question in his mind was where did he get that information from? Who wrote the note in the first place? Why would whoever had written it want the information to get to us?

Surely it was created to let us know about it. That meant that someone in China was very uncomfortable with what was happening and wanted us to do something.

He picked up his notes and walked over to the admiral's office.

He knocked at the door and was told to come in, Paul DeNice was sitting across from Admiral Walker and they were obviously looking over the outline Harold had prepared the other day.

Harold said, I believe we just got some answers to what you may be looking at.

He handed his notes to the admiral and said: "I just got a phone call from Carl Muskin. It seems that Dr. Lee sent an engagement card to his daughter, and in it, was a hand written note that she says was not written by her father.

"Carl and Lijuan both believe Dr. Lee doesn't know who gave him this note, but that whoever it was, they wanted us to know about it and used Dr. Lee as the messenger; knowing that Carl would call us."

Paul, who had taken the notes from Harold as he spoke, read through them. He looked up at Harold and said: "This is almost in code. How do we figure this?"

"He looked at the admiral and read aloud: '*The ocean waitress China Girl East is bringing a Suzhou dinner for the Honduras President, it should be there on December 14th, to Feed the Hungry Atom*'. The 'China Girl East', *i*sn't that the name of one of the ships owned by W.H. Shipping of Hong Kong?"

Harold said, "I think you are right, and I am sure the reference to Suzhou and the words '*Feed the Hungry Atom*', are a reference to the Tokomak site that Dr. Lee is the director of.

"Those items are a strong an indication that there is something being shipped to Honduras that we probably don't want shipped there."

Admiral Walker, who had remained quiet while Paul and Harold had gone over the note, spoke up and said: "Perhaps we need to look at what is actually stated in the note. What is apparently being shipped to Honduras, that is so important, is most likely some kind of nuclear device.

"That, my friends, is very serious, and would account for the high risk that both Dr. Lee, and whomever he got the information from, took!

"I think that it is time for both of you, Ira, Jane, Linda, and Luigi to sit down and go over the outline and everything we know and see if we have missed anything; and I think it is time for me to go over to the NSA and maybe also the state department and see if we can find a way to learn what is going on with this ship and it's cargo."

33

0800 Tuesday, 11 December 2018
Aboard the China Girl East,
1,644 Nautical Miles northwest of
the Panama, Canal

Captain Wo Chang stood on his bridge wing sipping his morning tea. It had been an uneventful ocean crossing so far, they had been averaging about twenty-four knots the whole way and the only problem had been some heavy weather as they passed north of the Islands by Okinawa. For the most part, the seas had been relatively smooth, and the ship stayed cleanly on course.

The course had brought them to within forty miles from the west coast of Mexico, where the west to east currents had turned southeast more towards Central America.

He calculated they would be at the Panama Canal on Thursday mid-morning. He had profiled his itinerary to the Panamanian Canal operations before he left Hong Kong, and it was within his schedule requirements.

He looked out at a large helicopter that was coming up on his stern and wondered who they were. It was a Mexican military helicopter, and as it flew alongside a large door opened and several Mexican Marines pointing guns at him made it clear that he was to stop.

Radio contact was established, and Captain Chang was told that under international agreements, Mexico was the controlling authority for the larger Central America Ocean region. He was then told that there would be a boarding party sent over for a document inspection and search for illegal drugs and or contraband.

The Mexican commander on the helicopter was polite but left no room for argument or protest from the Chinese captain.

Captain Chang was worried as he waited for the Mexican Marines to board his ship, for although he knew that there were occasional inspections in these waters, he hadn't expected it. He knew, of course, about the special isolated hold aboard his ship, but was unaware of its content. All the rest of his cargo was properly sealed and listed on his shipping manifest.

There had been stories of small ships, tramp freighters usually, who had resisted these inspections even to the point of scuttling and sinking their ships. It usually didn't end well for them.

Six Mexican Marines including an Officer boarded an inflatable raft, as the helicopter hovered, then came over to the boarding ladder that the ship's crew had lowered.

After polite introductions, the Captain and his eight-man crew were moved and kept together on the fore deck. The officer in charge took out his radio and called to the helicopter that all was under control.

About two minutes later, a large movement of water seventy-five yards off the 'China Girl East's' port side, had everyone looking at an American nuclear submarine as it surfaced. As it moved alongside, the sub's Captain called on the radio to the Mexican commander and asked to speak to the Chinese captain.

Once permission was given for the submarine to tie alongside, a U.S. Navy commander came aboard the Chinese freighter and told the Captain and crew that, under international agreements, commercial vessels were prohibited to transport nuclear materials.

He told the Captain, that information had been obtained that 'China Girl East' was probably in violation of that international agreement. The United States Navy, with its nuclear abilities, was asked by the Mexican government to determine if this was true and asked for permission to search the ship and cargo.

Although very polite and without any threat, there was no question that the search was mandatory. Captain Chang handed over to the Mexican commander the ships documents and stood aside.

The search of the cargo containers was perfunctory and quick; but the special access to the fore front hold was done very carefully. About an hour later, the four 'dirty bombs' that were in the hold, had been found sealed and transferred to the submarine.

The Ship was then officially seized by the Mexican government and ordered to sail to Santa Cruz for impound.

34

Thursday, December 13ᵗʰ, 9:00 a.m.,
The United Nations General Assembly
NYC

The General Secretary was positioned to speak to the General Assembly; to be followed by an address from Dr. Lee about the Suzhou Food Production Program.

The delegation, consisting of the General Secretary, Assistant Defense Secretary Chen Hui Sing, and Cabinet Officials, Liu Gen Feng, and General Dong Chao Jing, along with Dr. Lee; had arrived in the United States about noon the previous day. They were getting ready for the next day's program when they got word of the seizure of a Chinese commercial ship by Mexico.

The notification came from the General Secretary's office, but because it was a commercial ship, and was detained by Mexico, he decided to hold off on any formal complaint until more was known about it.

He passed the note to Minister Feng and said:

"Contact the American Secretary of State's office to let them know of this ship's detainment and ask if they have any knowledge of it. We will talk to the Mexican delegate later, when we know more about it."

The rest of the day was about recovering from a fifteen-hour flight and getting ready to address the General Assembly the next morning.

The next morning, upon the American Secretary of State's request, Assistant Defense Secretary Sing, Minister Feng, and General Jing, took a short flight to Washington for a preliminary meeting. It turned out to be much more than they expected.

After the meeting began, but before any discussion started, the American State department presented a video of the capture and removal of the 'dirty bombs' from the special hold aboard the 'China Girl East'.

The revelation was, of course, a surprise to everyone except General Jing. He, however, also showed surprise. The discussion between the two-high level undersecretaries proceeded for the next eight hours, with many phone calls to and from their own executive offices.

It was a serious breach of trust between the two countries, but neither wanted it to elevate into public conflict. China had come to America with an increased position of negotiating power over the Americans, and it had disappeared before it could even be discussed.

Surprisingly, neither the United States nor China wanted to downplay the improved food process program that Dr. Lee and CERN had brought forward to the world and wanted Dr. Lee to deliver it to the United Nations and the world as planned.

However, such a flagrant violation of nuclear responsibility, such as had occurred, could not be allowed to happen again.

Both the American Delegation, and the Chinese Delegation negotiations came to an agreement that was closer to what had been required by the United States; with a stronger USA exported food products to China and a decrease by about half of the USA tariffs imposed on Chinese goods imported to the USA.

There were additional terms discussed, of many items, that would ease tensions and result in better relations between the two world powers.

On the following day, Friday the 14th, after those discussions were complete; The American President and the Chinese General Secretary held a summit at Camp David near Washington, DC. Included was the signing of a new treaty that was good for both countries. At the following press conference, there was no mention of the Nuclear items or the seizure of a ship by Mexico.

The 'China Girl East', along with her crew, was released to continue her voyage, but without her special cargo. They had been cautioned, by the Chinese consulate and with approval of the Mexican representative, to avoid any comment whatsoever about their delay; simply discharge their cargo and return to Hong Kong. If pressed, simply say 'an engine problem'.

EPILOG

Saturday, December 15ᵗʰ, 1:00 p.m.,
University Chapel,
Central Texas University,
Austin, Texas

Dr. Lin Chang Lee, dressed in a formal tuxedo and a huge smile on his face, walked proudly down the aisle with his beautiful daughter Lijuan, hanging on his arm. Lijuan in a lovely all white wedding gown, carrying a bouquet of roses, was looking at her future husband who was smiling and waiting for her at the altar. Standing with Carl was his best man 1ˢᵗ Class Petty Officer Rudy O'Neil, and ahead of Lijuan and her father was Danielle Chartier from France, her maid of honor.

With the exchange of vows finished, and cheers from their guests, the newly wed couple almost ran back down the aisle.

On the grounds of the university, was a great French restaurant that Dr. Lee had reserved for the wedding reception.

The group of well-wishers was bigger than the young couple had originally figured, for there were both old and new friends that wanted to give them a great send off and all had been welcomed.

All of the archeological group from Syria had been excided to come, as were all of the rescue seal team members. In addition, about ten professors from CTU and several others from the local community were also there.

From NSIU in Washington, was Admiral Walker, Harold Jarrett, Jane McCalla, Paul DeNice and Linda DeSanto; all who had said they wouldn't miss it for the world.

A honeymoon in London for a week was the plan, and the flight was early the next morning.

Dr. Lee also had a flight, but not for three days. He had received permission to proceed to CERN in Switzerland and was excited to do so.

Admiral Walker decided to stay and spend some time with Dr. Lee; and was able to get tickets for them both at the CTU vs. Oklahoma football game the next day.

Back in Washington, Tuesday morning December 18th, Admiral Walker set up the closing discussion for the Suzhou Project Case. He called it to order in the third-floor conference room.

Present were all of the seal team members, Harold, Jane, Linda, Paul, and Ira.

The Admiral said: "This was a strange case on many levels, and we must use it to look to the future to assure we are always ready for the unusual.

"To begin with there was the satellite photos that first stirred our interest. As we all know, that developed into the Tokomak project; and as we learned of it, there was an unusual open presentation to the UN from the Chinese themselves.

"Harold, would you pick it up from here?"

Harold, picking up his notes, said: "Aye sir, Jane and I followed the trail and learned of Dr. Lee, CERN, and his proposed food enhancement project.

"I must admit that I, at least, had a hard time understanding just how this was going to change things. It was Linda, who by chasing a strange series of events, found the impact this could have on our Midwest farmers, and the shipping industry that was involved.

Linda picked up the narrative: "By luck, we found a few friends on Wall Street who knew all about the shipping and financial industries and explained the impact the China project might have.

"I suspect we may have been going down the wrong road had Harvey Wassel not picked that time to change his ocean shipping habits. His early change of routes moving them more to Asia service routes, opened the question of just what would be the impact on our food exports.

"Strangely, they hadn't changed. Perhaps it was just too early for the China food project to affect the market, but it opened competition among other ocean shipping companies."

Luigi spoke up: "I guess that this was about the same time that an absolute coincidence occurred with the DOD request for us to take out the terrorist cells in Syria.

"By just pure luck, we were able to rescue the archeologists before they were sacrificed. The romance between Carl and Lijuan, Dr. Lee's daughter, we all know well; but there is no doubt it worked in our favor."

Harold spoke up: "You are right Luigi, the relationship between Carl and Lijuan was soon endorsed by Dr. Lee; and he was ultimately the conduit for our learning about what was being done in Suzhou."

Admiral Walker said: "That brings us to the present, and what we now know about who and what was done.

"First, some of what I am telling you I learned this past Sunday from Dr. Lee. He is now more comfortable speaking about what happened than he was before.

"He told me that he was forced to allow a secret area at the Suzhou site that he wasn't aloud to see. He knew it was under camouflage cover and under continuous guard.

"He said that he was forced to allow it on his site or there would be insufficient funding for him to continue.

"It wasn't till he had found unusual radioactive readings on the grounds that he took the problem to Beijing. It was there that he learned that it was Defense Secretary Lieu who was in control of the secret project.

"He told me that he realized the Lieu didn't trust him and put a full surveillance team on everything he was doing. It was when he was on his way home from the Beijing meeting that he made the call to Carl; and it was before Lieu could get the surveillance started.

"We all know about the W.H. Shipping Company formation and it was through Harvey Wassel. We think when we have the FBI question Wassel about his Chinese contact, it will turn out to be Lieu.

"It will be up to the DOJ to determine if Wassel is to be charged, but with his money, who knows?

"To finish the outline, we do not know who gave Dr. Lee the note that he sent to Lijuan, knowing that Carl would get it to us. He and I both believe it was the intention of whoever it was to stop the nuclear interference in Central America from happening.

"It was successful. I just got a call from the State Department telling us that Secretary Lieu has been removed from his position, and that we will probably never see or hear of him again. He was replaced by General Dong Chao Jing, he served under Lieu but was known not to be a fan of his."

As the Admiral sat back and stretched, he said: "I think we did well, albeit there was a great deal of luck; and there is also no doubt that without the special connection between Lijuan and Carl Muskin, and Lijuan's father, we might never have known how close we were to a real disaster.

As he looked around at the people who made up this very special unit, he knew they all felt much the same. So, with a smile he added: "Unless anyone has anything else to add, I believe this meeting is adjourned!"